THE DRAGON ROSE UP OUT OF THE DESERT BEFORE HER...

The jeep skidded to a halt, half burying itself in the sand as the serpent raised its head, casting a shadow over Roxanna; its mouth gaped, its green eyes glowed like fiery gemstones, its long body writhed in the yellow sand. It seemed real enough to touch, but it had to be an illusion. *This cannot exist,* she insisted to herself, even as she watched it coil and breathe, blow sand and stir the air. *A hologram,* she decided. *With effects.*

To prove it to herself, she switched her jeep to manual control, hit the accelerator, and drove straight at the imaginary beast. And in the next horrifying instant she struck a substantial scaled body. . . .

THE WIND DANCERS

Wind Dancers

by
R. M. Meluch

A SIGNET BOOK
NEW AMERICAN LIBRARY

PUBLISHER'S NOTE

This novel is a work of fiction. Names, characters, places, and incidents are either the product of the author's imagination or are used fictitiously, and any resemblance to actual persons, living or dead, events, or locales is entirely coincidental.

COPYRIGHT © 1981 BY R. M. MELUCH

SIGNET TRADEMARK REG. U.S. PAT. OFF. AND FOREIGN COUNTRIES REGISTERED TRADEMARK—MARCO REGISTRADA HECHO EN CHICAGO, U.S.A.

SIGNET, SIGNET CLASSIC, MENTOR, PLUME, MERIDIAN AND NAL BOOKS are published by New American Library, 1633 Broadway, New York, New York 10019

FIRST PRINTING, MAY, 1981

3 4 5 6 7 8 9 10 11

PRINTED IN THE UNITED STATES OF AMERICA

To St. Jude

Wind Dancers

Part One:
AEOLIS

Aeolian Date 2/29/225   Earth Date 8/24/2378
Rain Forest, Little Asia, Northern, Aeolis

The wind howled like so many wild animals.

Then came a single voice, a mournful baying that swelled and died, as if to mark the passing of the Outcast One called Leader. Under the sheltering trees, where the air was still and the wind was felt only as a voice, the dying man lay in the arms of his younger follower, the one called Pala. And around them a small ring of the Outcast kept vigil.

Pala cradled the frail body close to him and leaned his head against the whitened hair. He could feel Leader trying to breathe, each inhalation a painful effort. The young Outcast felt the pain as if it were his own, and he shut his eyes tight, a shimmer of moisture on his thin lashes.

Abruptly the old man's breath caught, and a razor of fear tore through Pala. But then the wheezing exhalation followed, and another gasp. There were still a few moments left.

They were huddled at the foot of a precipice in the dark of a tropical forest. Nearby, a thin column of water falling from the towering cliff pierced the vast green canopy of the trees and allowed a space where one might see the sky. Down through this window peered the three moons, named by the Earthlings Kushuh, Dattas, and Tarŭ, strung in an arc across

1

the sky, one waxing, one full, one waning, all shrouded in wispy clouds and mist that shifted before a restless wind. The Ancient Ones were said to have read something important from the moons, but what it was no one now could tell.

Pala gazed up at them with blurred vision, searching in desperation for some sign, someone to tell him what to do.

A light touch on his wet cheek startled him, and an unsteady voice very close to his ear said, "Do not cry for me, Pala. I am very relieved to be going at last."

Pala looked down into Leader's eyes, which were dull-focused, perhaps unable to see him at all. "Please don't die," Pala begged him. "Save yourself."

"For what?" Leader asked with great calm. "To become an Outcast Old One? Do not wish that on me. That is my vision of what the Earthlings call hell. No, dearest of all to me, let me go."

His face was serene, a shadow of sorrow crossing his brow, but no fear. He felt very light to hold, fragile as a bird. Of his former strength there was none.

Pala bowed his head to hide his face against Leader's chest. "Who will lead us now?" he wept.

A trembling hand lifted his face, and Leader told him very softly, "You will."

"Not me!" Pala cried. His voice, which never rose above a whispering rush, broke with attempted volume. "Oh no, not me!"

"You are eldest," said Leader. "And you are not a criminal. You were not cast out for that. There is no one else."

"But I—" Pala stammered, tears of fear mixing with tears of grief. "I don't *know* anything."

"Do you think I do?" Leader said sadly. "There are no passed-down secrets. If there were any, they have been lost. The only requirement for being Leader is to have the misfortune to be picked by the last one." He smiled with tender pity. "And that misfortune has fallen on you."

He stopped to rest, wearied from the effort of speaking.

Moaning, the wind that was vanguard of a storm rippled through the treetops. Pala was shaking.

At last Leader took a few breaths and said, "Do not fear. You will find strength when you need it. . . . Be good, little Pala, even though you are Outcast. The Ancient Ones and the Old Ones have been known to forgive. What you are is not your fault," said Leader. He inhaled, and exhaled a sigh. "Your time will be hard. You will preside over the end."

"No!" Pala tried to cry out, but no sound came. He could not bear the thought of being the last one left.

"There will be no more children," Leader said, resigned. "It is a pity that we do not pay only for our own mistakes. . . . Remember to avoid the Earthlings. They fear what they do not understand. Don't let them know we are here. It should not be difficult—they are trying so very hard not to know." He closed his eyes. "Those are the only words I can give you. . . . Burn my body. Don't just bury it. I don't want the robots to find me."

Pala tried to speak, tried to call him Leader, but what came out was *Awan*—"Father" in the Ancient tongue.

Eyes still shut, Leader smiled—

—and was suddenly overcome by a fit of coughing, brittled ribs heaving in spasms. He jerked forward out of Pala's arms, the veins in his neck standing out in strain.

Then he fell back against Pala, breathless, face white, one eye awash with red where a blood vessel had broken. He took one last breath and spoke in a whisper. "Give me a kiss now. You were like kin of mine."

Pala pressed his lips to the aged forehead that already felt cold, and, when he drew back, the wheezing breath had ceased.

He closed the blank staring eyes and gently brushed the blood from the lid of the one. Then he sobbed, half in loss, half in the knowledge that his title was no longer Pala.

Finally he was forced to regard the other Outcast standing over him, looking at him as if he should tell them what to do.

"Um," he began, trying to think. An order. He was supposed to give them an order. "Build a pyre."

That one was easy—he had been told to say that. From here he would have to give his own commands.

He carefully laid the body on the soft ground, and moved away from the others to sit awhile alone.

The place he came to was under the window to the sky where the breezes swept down the cliff face along with the waterfall. He sat on a wet rock and shivered.

Brown eyes that could see in the dark settled on beads of water rolling off the ferns at the streamside. And he watched with all his attention to forget for a moment what he was, a small boy-man with a whispery voice, whom the Outcast now called Leader.

3/1/225 *Ledges,*
New Africa, Southern, Aeolis

Morning. A Gathering.

The place to which the Outcast had come was called the Ledges. Here the evidence of Earthling presence which pervaded the rest of the world was absent. None of their buildings stood here, and there was no trace of their plantlife that now grew everywhere else. This place alone remained untouched.

The Earthlings had transformed Aeolis from a barren world of wind and soil into a living paradise, a spacious garden for their extremely wealthy to enjoy. In such alien surroundings, the Outcast felt like stowaways on a beautiful ship. They knew they should not be there, but there was nowhere else to go. Home no longer existed, not as it had been. The only place they almost belonged was the Ledges. This the Earthlings had not made. The wind, water, and sand of Aeolis had created the Ledges.

The cliffs and canyons ran on as far as the jagged skyline and beyond. Naked rock had been wind-blasted into towers over a kilometer high, majestic arches that spanned the entire width of a canyon, and infinite varied shapes, some at peace, stately and cathedrallike, some almost mobile in their violence, the savagely lovely work of a tortured artist.

The Ledges supported no life, but it was as beautiful as any wooded or grassy place the Earthlings had cultivated. And because it was not alive it seemed a fitting place to bring the dead to rest—a place where the Earthlings' robots did not patrol, so the grave might not be defiled.

The robots were omnipresent. The planet was honeycombed with tunnels for the machines programmed as caretakers of the man-made paradise, keeping the fragile life-web in perfect balance.

The Outcast were not part of that balance. They were not supposed to exist. They managed to keep their existence secret because there were so few of them—only twenty-four now—and most of those looked startlingly similar to the Earthlings.

The Outcast's animals were a different matter. Some bore vague resemblances to Earth animals, but none of them could actually pass for one. Fortunately for the Outcast, the sightings of their animals were invariably passed off as imagination, illusion, hoax, or hallucination.

Hence, the Outcast remained undetected—or at least ignored—by the Earthlings.

However, the dead bodies of the Ancient Ones in the desert were not so easily explained or ignored.

Alive, the Ancient Ones avoided detection altogether. But once dead, unlike the Outcast, there was no one to bury them, so their bodies were left to be found. Yet as they were discovered—usually by robots—they were quietly collected, disposed of, and never mentioned, never inquired into.

The Earthlings were indeed trying very hard not to know that they were not alone on the planet Aeolis.

And because they were trying so hard, no one liked to imagine what they would do if they found out for certain that they were sharing their world.

The new Leader of the Outcast looked around the funeral ring at twenty-two of his twenty-three followers who should not exist. These were the Outcast come to bury the charred remains of One-Who-Had-Been-Leader. All of them had come but one.

"Where is Leo?" Leader whispered.

The ring met him with silence.

"Did anyone tell him?" he asked.

"He was told," the seven voices of the seven Ones called Pleiades, mistresses of seven white dogs, sounded in unison.

Then where is he?

The sun was already nearing the horizon, and it would soon be light. Mild panic gnawed at Leader. Though he loved the light, he was physically suited to darkness, and if he stayed out much longer the day that followed would blind him.

As he waited for missing Leo, his eyes settled on Scorpii, who should have been crying but was not. She had been the old Leader's companion. Not a wife, but sometimes a lover.

She was naked like all the rest of them, sitting cross-legged in the ring with sullen sensuality, her thick dark hair covering her like a veil. The crime that made her Outcast had been her mating outside her scorpion caste. Since then she had gone on to Earthmen despite the taboo. But none of what she did was for pleasure. That part was of no matter. Anything Scorpii ever did was out of desire for children.

She would have none. Not when the last of their kind consisted of seventeen females and seven sterile males.

Her dark eyes were locked on the bundle in the center of the ring that contained the remains of her dead lover, the one she had been most faithful to, and in her eyes was not sorrow, but resentment, for he had left her here without child.

Leader shivered at Scorpii's cold stare, and he looked away toward the horizon.

He waited till the sun touched the rocks and the dawn was on fire. Leo was not coming.

"Let us begin," Leader said, taking his place in the ring between Pega and Basilisk as he always did.

"No, you have it wrong," someone objected before he could even start.

It was Draco, eyes turned toward him, small black eyes that never blinked.

"What is it?" asked Leader, hand on his brow to shade out the light.

"An error in procedure," Draco explained with a kind of demented merriment, leering with thin red lips and rising like a serpent uncoiling.

A day dweller, his sun-baked skin leathery brown, Draco crossed through the middle of the ring to Leader. "One-Who-Was-Pala, our leader does not belong in the ring with us," Draco hissed, enjoying himself. "We need an elevated position for him."

And, with that, Draco seized the startled Leader with a strong, deceptively thin arm, and carried him up the rocks to a ledge overlooking the ring. There Draco set him down.

"Now you look like a leader," he said. "Sort of."

From this vantage, above the others, the full impact of Leader's changed status was brought home to him, One-Who-Was-Pala, and he cried, "No! Not me! Oh, God, not me!"

Draco smirked. "We have no god. You are beginning to sound like an Earthman." And he laughed, not because there was anything funny, but because there was not much else to do. "Continue now. I will catch you if you become confused again," Draco said and scrambled down from the ledge to the ring.

And Leader stopped protesting. There was no use. He was trapped with his loathsome new title and all it implied. It was time to accept what he was and to bury the dead. The day was growing brighter, and the ring was waiting for him to speak.

"We have come to lay to rest the One-Who-Had-Been-Leader," he began in a whisper, feeling as though he were burying himself. "Is there anyone here who knew his name?"

It was a ritual question he had to ask, though he knew the answer. Only kin and spouse could know one's real name; all others called one by his title.

None of the Outcast had family living. None were married. None *could* marry, being all of different castes.

No one answered the question.

"Then there will be no marker," said Leader very sadly. "No family shroud."

And since there were no relatives to be put at ease, the rite would be very brief, a simple, short farewell.

Leader spoke the ritual words. "Rest now, one we knew as Leader. Your time with us is at an end. Be at peace with your ancestors."

Then, too numb to cry, he added the lines that had become traditional for the Outcast: "May the Ancient Ones and the Old Ones acknowledge you and not maintain your exile past the grave, for who can hold grudges against the dead?"

And that was all. He invoked no deity, for they had none.

The bones were laid in a shaded grave beneath the cliffs with the words "Never stir," and then covered over.

Free to go, the Outcast lingered a few moments, caught by a sense of something unfinished.

The Pleiades were first to leave, and a howling of seven dogs could be heard echoing through the Ledges.

Pega's animal appeared briefly, a white equine creature with lion's mane, cleft hoofs, and a beard like a goat's. She lacked the power and mass of a horse, quick and graceful instead. She looked as though she belonged to an Earth fairy tale, a unicorn without a horn, Pegasus without wings. She tossed her narrow, wedge-shaped head, and darted over the dry land, weaving among the rocks and out of view.

The rest disbanded, drifting in their own directions, till only a small knot remained, Leader, Little Bird, and Draco, hovering about the grave.

It was then that Leo appeared, his inhuman face beaded with sweat, all his ribs showing in his panting sides. He ran up to the new Leader and spoke his message as if he could fling it from himself and hide. "The Service is here."

Leader gaped, stupidly silent, his brain refusing to comprehend. He had been prepared to be furious, to vent his grief on Leo. In fact he was prepared for anything but this.

The Earth military Service had not been on Aeolis in ages, certainly not in recent memory. Its return could mean only one thing. "They are after us," said Draco.

"Not us . . . not exactly," Leo backtracked, whiskers twitching in agitation. "They are here because of the Ancient Ones—because of their bodies in the desert. It is the Ancient Ones' fault the Service is here."

"But what can the Ancient Ones do?" Leader said in resignation. "Stop dying?"

"They don't have to die the way they do," Draco spoke acidly. "The Service may have come because of the Ancient Ones, but if the Service finds anyone, it won't be the Ancient Ones. It will be *us*."

Leader placed both hands over his eyes, to block out the light, to block out thought. He cried, not really speaking to anyone, "But I thought the Earthlings were trying to ignore us."

Draco regarded him with contempt. "Then evidently," he countered, blinkless eyes glittering malevolently, "they are not trying hard enough."

Chapter II.
Roxanna

Commander Roxanna Douglas drove her Service jeep between star dunes down a long flat corridor of sand. Veils of clouds tinted violet drifted across the desert sky and it might have been raining, but no water touched the ground, for it evaporated again in the parched air even as it fell.

Though the commander was a bit leery of her present assignment with its morbid overtones, she could not find fault with the surroundings—so much *space* and so incredibly beautiful. She had never conceived of this kind of wealth—and wealth in the most concrete of forms, land. For the first time in her life she looked to the horizon of an Earth-owned world where absolutely no one else was in sight. She propped her feet up on the dashboard and raised her arms to the dry wind. "Do you believe this?" she said and laughed. She was talking to her bagpipes, which lay in the back seat. Disturbed by a current of air, they moaned as if in response.

She folded her hands behind her head and steered the jeep with one booted foot.

Commander Douglas was an attractive woman, slender and trim, though considered hopelessly low-class on a world such as Aeolis—an acceptable lackey, perhaps. Her auburn brows, over auburn eyes, were thick, arched, and untamed, bordering on bushy, though the rest of her features were very fine. Her auburn hair was cut off straight at chinlength, her bangs held off her forehead by a pair of decorative pins that were not exactly regulation. Under her black Service uniform jacket she wore a vest of the Douglas tartan, which was not

9

regulation either. Plugged into the back of her head at the base of her skull was a regulation language nodule, a small plastic box of man-made brain that enabled her to understand her Swedish captain, her Chinese-Balinese lieutenant, and the people of various nationalities she encountered at different ports of call.

This particular port she was in no hurry to leave, and she hoped their mission would fail so she would be stationed here indefinitely.

What Commander Douglas and the Serviceship *Halcyon XLV* were supposed to be doing on Aeolis was getting rid of the people who did not belong here.

But first they had to find them.

The police had never caught one of these people, had no idea who they were or how they got here, and the only reason anyone knew such people existed at all was that they died here—alone, old, naked, and without an ID in the known galaxy. The police called them Morts.

The first mystery was how there could be any such thing as an unidentified being.

All Earthlings and intelligent beings allied with Earth were catalogued in the Universal Bank Computer. It was said that it was easier for one to be born without his mother noticing than to escape detection by the UBC.

The second puzzle was even more baffling: How did these people, the Morts, come to be on Aeolis?

The planet was called Aeolis by its discoverers because it was "nothing but wind" when they found it, with no trace of anything organic—and certainly no Morts. Yet there was nitrogen in the soil and oxygen in the atmosphere despite the lack of vegetation; and Aeolis was deemed the perfect place to transform into an Eden. So a world with only desirable life had been designed—a planet free of disease, free of vermin, its balance kept by other means than undesirable predators. It was a fragile world, and was by necessity the most regulated planet in the galaxy. Smuggling was an impossibility, and stowing away an absurdity. Nothing passed the inspection station on the inner moon, Kushuh, without being checked, cleared, and catalogued. Not even a microorganism.

So, if the Morts were not on the planet to begin with, and there was no way for them to be brought in, then how did they happen to be there?

The third puzzle was *why*. There was a rhyme but no reason. All the Morts were naked, had apparently died of natural causes; most of them were found in uninhabited areas—like the desert—and all were discovered on this particular planet. But why?

Whatever the answers, the officers of the *Halcyon XLV* realized that the sooner Aeolis was rid of the Morts the better. Not only did they represent a very real threat of smuggling in something uncontrollable, like a virus, but the fear that they evoked carried in its wake a predictable influx of human jackals and the resurgence of old Aeolian horror stories from the pioneer days—impossible tales of witches and ghosts, or even dragons and werewolves.

Stupid, frightened people, Roxanna was thinking with mild contempt, her jeep headed toward the setting sun, when the dragon rose up out of the desert before her.

From reflex she threw one arm up to shield her face, jerked her feet off the dash, and fumbled for the brake, her throat constricting with unreasoning fear.

The jeep skidded to a halt, half-burying itself in the sand, as the serpent raised its head, casting a shadow over Roxanna, its mouth gaping, green eyes glowing like fiery gemstones, its long body writhing in the yellow sand, real enough to touch, though it had to be an illusion.

Resisting the impulse to turn in panicked flight, Roxanna pushed back her hair in a jerky nervous motion and narrowed her auburn eyes at the moving silhouette between herself and the sun. Her small mouth was drawn in a hard line as she fought down an instinctive fear which came over her with a heated wave of heavy reptilian smell that threatened to make her forget what she knew: *This cannot exist.*

Yet it coiled and breathed, blew sand, stirred the air, and stank as if to insist it must exist.

A hologram, she decided. *With effects.*

To prove it to herself, she switched her jeep to manual control, hit the accelerator, and drove straight at the beast.

And struck a substantial scaled body.

The front of the jeep buckled, and she was thrown out as it turned over.

3/2/225 Oasis Port,

Desert of the Bells, Northern, Aeolis

I am going mad.
Roxanna could not remember ever feeling so humiliated, frustrated, and helpless. Her broken bones had been mended before she had even awakened, so there was no reason for what she said to be dismissed as concussion-induced delirium. But it was.

Her captain, Per Safir, was throwing darts at a target hung on the ship's bulkhead, unconcerned by her collision—in fact, tickled that Roxanna's infernal bagpipes had been crushed. Unlike her bones, her bagpipes had not been repaired.

The ship's lieutenant, Buddy Tsai, whom Roxanna could usually count on as an ally, remained in uncomfortable, dubious silence. He was still wearing his medical nodule and was busily logging the report of Roxanna's injuries into the computer.

Roxanna stood indignantly behind Per, out of the path of his darts, her fists jammed into the pockets of her black trousers. She was barefoot, her white shirt half-buttoned, the sleeves rolled up. She wore her hat at a rakish, nonregulation angle because she knew it irritated her captain. If she stood there long enough, Per was bound to become nervous and either miss his aim or be forced to talk to her.

Finally he spoke without looking at her, without taking his eyes from the dartboard. "It was a mirage, Roxy." He let a dart fly. It bit into the crowded bull's-eye on the far side of the compartment.

"Mirages don't have shadows," said Roxanna.

"Lots of things besides dragons do, though," said Per, taking aim again.

"All right then, you tell me what I hit," she said to his back. "In the middle of wide-open nothing, tell me what I hit. I didn't crash my jeep into *wind.*"

Per's dart rebounded off the metal rim of the target. Per Safir never hit the rim.

He stopped, turned to Roxanna in irritation, and said, "I don't know. There was no sign of anything on or around the jeep."

Roxanna bit her lip. Surely she had hit the beast hard

enough to draw blood, or at least scrape off a few scales. The wind must have sand-blasted the jeep clean.

"And there was no sign of dragons," Per continued dryly. He had stalked across the compartment and was pulling his darts from the board, glancing downward all the while, hesitant to pick up the stray one from the deck. Finally he bent down with a look of wounded dignity and retrieved it. Then he looked at Roxanna directly, his eyes green as the serpent's. "Roxy, you know better. There is nothing remotely *resembling* a dragon here. There are no big snakes. There aren't even any *little* snakes. There aren't any snakes at all."

Here Buddy Tsai looked up from the computer console and added, "There aren't even any big caterpillars."

That was supposed to be funny, but Roxanna did not laugh. She couldn't—not when she thought she was going mad yet *knew* she was not.

3/2/225 Cave of the Winds,

Ledges, New Africa, Southern, Aeolis

"I want to kill," Draco said.

"Hush." Leader's voice rushed and whispered in the Cave of the Winds.

The rock chamber was illumined with shafts of light that performed a slow shifting dance as day progressed, and from their position one could tell the day was still young in this part of the world.

One ray fell across the surface of a subterranean pool in which Leader was regarding his reflection, the image of a slight creature with the pale skin of a night dweller who shied from the sun—and was afraid to close his eyes in darkness. Leader reached down and touched the water to blur the image.

When the ripples cleared, the image reformed with Draco standing over his shoulder, murder in his eyes. Their gazes met in the mirror surface. "Sit," said Leader.

Too upset to think about disobeying, Draco seated himself, cowed and angry. He made one more attempt to arouse fear and awe in his audience of one. "The dragon kills tonight," he said.

"You know who brought this on you," said Leader quietly. "Now let it be."

Draco glowered at him, each muscle in his face set into a cruel sinuous line.

Then he shocked Leader by starting to cry. "But my dragon might die," Draco whimpered, voice small as a child's.

Draco had not expected the driver of the jeep to charge at his beast like that. Everyone else sped away in delightfully comic horror whenever he pulled that trick. But Draco had never before dealt with the Service. "I was only trying to help."

He coiled himself into a fetal ball, his head down, his coarse hair brushing the bedrock floor. The dragon was all Draco had except his life, and without the dragon his life was not much.

Tentatively, Leader reached out as if to a creature that might bite. No one had ever told Leader not to pet wounded animals.

He lightly placed his palm on the leatherlike skin of Draco's back—and immediately felt hard muscles contract under his hand.

Draco raised his head, his eyes dry. "You thought I was crying, didn't you."

"I thought so," said Leader.

"I wasn't."

Leader sighed. "Let the dragon rest. It may yet recover if you let it." He motioned toward the dark recesses of the inner cave. "In there."

Draco's thin lips twitched. He paused, wanting to give in but not wanting to look as if he was giving in. "Only because the dragon is tired," said Draco. "But *then* it will kill," he assured Leader and made his way deeper into the cave.

Leader heard the dragon settle and breathe a heavy pained sigh.

One crisis passed. Leader supposed it was safe to assume that now.

But it left him facing a far graver crisis. The Service. It was a Servicewoman who had struck the dragon. The Service would have to know about them now.

Leader pulled a blanket around himself and leaned back against the rock wall, waiting for the worst.

The wind whistled a musical chord as it passed through several of the crevices in the cave. The light rays changed pattern, faded, and disappeared as night came on.

After a while the windsong in the rocks ceased, leaving only the sound of water dripping into the underground pool, and the sound of quiet breathing.

Leader could no longer see. He had overstayed one too many dawns outside and now his night sight was gone. One day he would blind himself entirely and spend the rest of his life in the darkness he dreaded.

He sensed someone else had entered the cave. By the silent, sure movements he knew it must be Leo, his fellow exile of the light—except that Leo loved the dark in which he could hide his face. Leo had never burned his eyes in full daylight.

Leo came to Leader's side and crouched next to him, grasping his forearm with icy hands to let him know where he was.

Leo was the one who watched, a prowler, a stalker, a hider, a seeker, the one who knew where the spaceport was at which the Service ship had landed. In the dark his breathing sounded frantic, but it was hard to tell if he were bearing bad news, for Leo was *always* frightened.

When Leader spoke, it was in his lowest whisper. "The Service knows?"

"No," Leo said. "No one believes the woman. They think she's *haatti*."

Haatti—moon-mad. All the Outcast used the ancient word, though none could say what madness had to do with the moons.

"They *don't* know?" said Leader, unable to believe.

"In spite of Draco," said Leo, with no attempt at kindness.

"Hush," Leader whispered urgently, lest the dragon awaken to the sound of a hated voice.

But Leo was oblivious to Draco's presence and to Leader's warning. "The dragon is dying now, at least. You've gotten your wish."

"I never said that," said Leader.

"You said you would like to see it gone—"

"I didn't! I—" Leader stammered in panic.

"You said you wished there were no more dragons—"

"Not the same!"

"What is wrong with you? I'm on *your* side—"

And that was the last thing that needed saying. From the darkest part of the cave, where even Leo could not see, they could hear a hiss and the sound of scales scratching rock, something very large uncoiling, unseen.

Then the sound of water disturbed.

"Draco!" Leader called into the utter blackness in the loudest voice he could manage. "You aren't moving that beast—"

He felt his way over the limestone on his hands and knees, scraped his chin on rock as his hand plunged into deep cold water. He had found the pool, under the surface of which was the cave's only entrance large enough for a man—or a dragon. "Draco, are you still here?"

He cocked his head and listened, but he and Leo were the only ones he heard. "Oh, Leo, he's gone."

"Good," said Leo.

"But he's going to kill."

The last time the serpent had gone on a rampage, it had slaughtered a herd of Arabian horses and left ripped carcasses strewn in pieces across the pasture and painted the fields around red with their blood. Luckily for the Outcast, the Earthlings had thought it the work of a deranged Earthman. Leader wondered if they would be so lucky now.

Leo was not worried. "What do you think a dying dragon has strength enough to kill?" he said coldly.

Only an animal without fangs or claw or hoof.

Leader did not want to think.

3/2/225 Des Vaux Estate,

Forêt Noir, New Europe, Northern, Aeolis

The serpent uncoiled, coiled, rearranged the long loops of its body, keeping its wound off the ground. Its head swayed in time with the throbbing pain in its side. Strident voices lanced its nerves. It moved toward the sound.

Seen between the trees, a man and woman, both black as predawn darkness, became the focus of pain. The man was running away from the angry woman, who stood on the marble steps of the mansion, screaming down curses.

The serpent emerged from the woods, jaws opening.

The woman's eyes rounded, voice stopped, and she pointed. The man turned, shrieked.

Mouth engulfed the man, then closed with snapping of bones and spurt of blood between its teeth.

The beast lowered its body to lie full length on the ground, then swallowed, the faintest bulge forming in its neck behind its blood-spattered head. Then it slithered into the woods.

By the time the police arrived—within the minute—the serpent had vanished without a trace.

3/2/225 *Cave of the Winds,*

Ledges, New Africa, Southern, Aeolis

It was still night when Draco returned to the Cave of the Winds, but the reflecting faces of two moons cast a faint light through the crevices, and he could be seen as a moving shape. He wrapped Leader's blanket around his shoulders and curled into himself, chuckling with a touch of hysteria that might have become tears. He broke out with a wild cackle, stifled it, and giggled to himself.

Leader knelt before him, thinking the unthinkable, his usually brown eyes dilated to total blackness. "Draco, what have you done?"

Draco licked his lips with dry red tongue.

"Draco!" Leader's voice cracked.

Draco's eyebrows lifted and lowered over changeless eyes. "Munch crunch went the bones. Squish drip went the blood." And he dissolved into giggles.

"What bones?" Leader demanded, trembling. "What blood?"

"*Whose* bones," said Draco. "*Whose* blood."

"It *ate* someone!" Leader tried to shriek in horror, but it came out a hoarse rasp.

Draco nodded, madly pleased. "Do not fear," he said. "It wasn't a Service officer."

Not sure if that was intended as reassurance or mockery, and not really caring, Leader sank back on his heels, sick and dizzy, letting go of Draco's shoulders. "The Ancient Ones and the Old Ones will never ever forgive us."

"The Ancient Ones and the Old Ones are dead," said Draco.

"They are more alive than we," said Leader, tears on his face.

"*They*," Draco said, leaning forward, eyes wide and maniacal, "can't *eat*!" And he doubled over, shrieking with laughter.

3/3/225 *Des Vaux Estate,*
New Europe, Northern, Aeolis

The grounds were deserted. Roxanna Douglas approached the mansion with a vague sense of unease, trying to pinpoint why exactly the Des Vaux estate felt so *dead*.

Slight aberrations in the usual Aeolian perfection unsettled her: a dead leaf caught in the delicate filigree of the wrought-iron gate; windfallen debris collecting on the still waters of a pool of lotus; autumn catkins and maple keys scudding across the walk, unswept. Had all the caretaker robots been turned off?

There was no sign of servants or footmen. No one came to meet her or to challenge her approach. She seemed to be the only conscious life on this estate. Where was everyone?

It was not possible, was it, that the police had already come and taken the marquise away? Roxanna wanted to talk to the woman who had seen the dragon.

She stopped by a marble pier, pulled the brass ring in a stone lion's mouth, and suddenly there were birds in the air, images of swallows that had already gone for the winter, and the sound of their recorded trilling and of crickets that were actually too cold to sing.

Roxanna turned the brass ring again and the birds vanished. The estate was silent again, deserted, dead, slightly disturbed.

Her skin prickled with the sense of something very, very wrong. She could hear her own heart beat in the silence.

The police could *not* have come yet. So where was the marquise?

"Hello?" Roxanna broke the empty stillness. "I'm not the police. Please don't shoot. Is anyone here?"

There was no answer, no stirring, so she trotted up to the marble porch with quick steps, seized both brass rings on the double doors, and rapped loudly.

The sound echoed within the dark house.

Roxanna stepped away from the door and looked for monitors, but they were too well disguised to be found. And probably dark anyway.

She jumped off the porch into the flower bed to have a look through a window.

To see a woman inside crumpled on the floor.

Oh, dear God, no. Lady, you didn't.

Roxanna leaped back onto the porch, yanked at the brass door handles. *Please be alive. Please. Please.* But the doors were locked.

She bounded back into the garden, tried the windows, then finally seized up a rose-granite squirrel that decorated the garden and hurled it through the glass. Her jacket wrapped around one arm, her face hidden in the crook of her other arm, she cleared the window frame, then took a short running start, vaulted inside, lunged across the room, and fell to her knees to touch the motionless woman's neck and feel for a pulse that was not there.

She sat back on her muddy heels, numb, her galloping heartbeat calming to a dull thudding.

Damn.

This must have been the marquise.

Roxanna gently turned the body over, and an image flickered in the air to one side. Roxanna looked up to face a hologram of the most majestic human being she had ever seen in her life. It was hard to believe the woman in the image and the broken husk on the floor were one and the same. But they were.

Even Aeolis's duchess did not look so regal.

The lady in the hologram stood fully two meters high. On her head was a tiara with a short chain of gold rings intertwined with a ringlet of black hair hanging down from one side to her shoulder. A tiny star ruby sat high on her cheek, and a gold ring pierced one nostril of her wide nose. She stood in royal immobility.

Then large, slanted, startlingly-violet eyes opened. The image's full lips moved and a recording sounded in a voice that was deep, smooth, and angry, with the capacity to become shrill and piercing, speaking the last words of the marquise Des Vaux.

"You will find my will in order," the dead woman's image

said. "I trust you will carry it out, for you cannot try me post-humously and I shall be dead by the time you hear this. This seemed the only way to preserve my rights as a human being. I am not a criminal and I will not be taken from my home as a captive. I will say this once more, and you must believe it, for the law says you must as this is my dying testimony: I did not kill my husband. I wish I had. Life would be much simpler. For now it is impossible."

And the voice went silent. The image remained, frozen in proud despair.

Roxanna knelt awhile in sorrow, fury, pity, disgust, till sunlight breaking through the autumn clouds streamed in the broken window, paled the hologram, and caught on pieces of shattered glass in the room.

Roxanna looked from the faded image to what remained of the woman who had been of a proud aristocratic breed so overrefined she hadn't the strength to live and fight.

I know you're telling the truth. I'll prove it for you. I only wish I'd done it sooner. It's too late for you, but not for your memory.

And not for me.

There were two people already destroyed by the serpent. Roxanna did not intend to be the third. She was not of the weak breed. Mongrels were tough to kill, and this she knew for a fact: *I am not going mad.*

Chapter III.
Laure

3/8/225 Remington Estate,
New Africa, Southern, Aeolis

East.

Crushed hat in hand, he stood in the parlor of the Remington house, waiting to meet the lady.

No one knew East's given name, and he never volunteered the information. He was an aging bachelor who played poker for blood, shot a sad game of pool, and smoked cigarettes, preferred cigars but could not afford them. He had lost a leg in a hunting accident, and the new leg sometimes gave him pain, so he sometimes drank too much alcohol. He was one of relatively few men who still bothered shaving his face instead of having the growth stopped until such time as he wanted a beard. He was a veteran of the Service and onetime crewmate of Roxanna Douglas, who would be happy if their paths did not cross again while both happened to be on the same planet. He was, in her eyes, something paleolithic. She was not surprised that he was still unmarried, and she suspected if he ever found a wife it would be by dragging one into a cave by her hair.

East rarely regretted never marrying. Occasionally he felt a pang of loss when he saw a man with a child who looked just like him, or a woman holding a baby. Attractive women by themselves made him think of other things than marriage.

There were women enough—more and prettier as he grew older, which he did not understand, but he did not complain.

His record, for the most part, was clear, the idiocies of youth having been deleted after years of good behavior, except for one crime of forty years ago that could never be erased.

It had actually been an accident during a barroom brawl, but the fact that East had been trained in unarmed combat and should have been in control made it murder. The sentence had been twenty-five years in the Service, during which he killed five more men legally. East was now a private citizen, had been ever since his sentence was up, a veteran who had learned to keep his temper very well.

Normally a man like East would have no business on Aeolis, but since the disappearance of the marquis Des Vaux, whether eaten by a dragon or murdered by someone who created the idea of a dragon, East had been hired by an Aeolian lord to protect his lady.

Lord Stephen Remington was a pleasant blond pacifist. Despite his strong features and stature, he struck East as a fundamentally weak man. Not only did Lord Stephen lack the bearing of a man who owned the ground on which he walked, but he gave the impression that whoever he borrowed it from would repossess it at any given moment.

"I am not a violent man," he had explained to East. His voice should have been rich and resonant, but his breath was shallow and he talked from his throat. Were he ever to become excited while speaking, East was certain Lord Stephen would strangle. "Were it just myself I would take my chances," the lord had said. "I could harm no one, not even to save myself. But I must think of my wife. I must protect her from the predators that have invaded Aeolis."

So you imported a predator of your own, thought East as the lord went to find his wife.

East sensed himself something of a curiosity as he stood in the parlor by the stair, waiting for the lady. He was aware of servants staring at him as they went about their duties. Slowly he figured out what about his appearance was so startling to them: everyone else on Aeolis was pretty. By birth or by human intervention, they were all flawless. Even the servants were ornamental, as they were status symbols rather than purely functional assets, for robots were more efficient and far less expensive. East, however, had let himself age and was an eyesore. He guessed he had the only wrinkles and scars on all of Aeolis.

He let the servants stare.

Lady Laure was upstairs, hiding from her husband and the new hireling, her ex-convict bodyguard. A different kind of servant, in some situations *he* could give orders to *her*. The prospect was interesting, though not altogether to her liking. She knew he had arrived—she could hear his strong deep voice—but still she did not go down.

Never let anyone think you wait for him. Be waited for, be waited on, but never wait. Her mother, when she was still alive, had taught her that.

She heard her husband come up the lift, go down the hall to her empty room—

"Laure."

—down the lift, throughout the house—

"Laure?"

—onto the veranda and outside.

On hearing the doors close behind him, she crept out of hiding and came halfway down the stairs, expecting to see someone dashingly handsome. So she was startled when she saw East waiting in the parlor.

Couldn't be, yet had to be. He was the homeliest human being she had ever seen in her sheltered life. She had known he was old, but she had not expected him to *look* it. His face was beginning to sag with middle-aged wrinkles, and he was dressed like a shabby commoner. He held in one hand a hat that looked as if it had been sat on. It had. And though he might barely have the height, he was too thin. Where were the big muscles of a bodyguard like those that watched over the duchess? It could not be.

Yet the sureness, the almost arrogance of his bearing, unintimidated by the opulent surroundings, like one who does not know inferiority, the piercing sharpness of the blue eyes, these qualities belonged to the man she would have protect her. Despite the rumpled clothing she could detect a bodily strength. He was not as bulky as she had expected, but hard and lean. And the scars on his face—one on his cheek, one over his eyebrow—who else would have scars? Had to be.

After she was done being shocked and disappointed, she was intrigued. Her preconception, she decided, was all wrong. This was what East should look like. Tall and thin, silver hair, sharp blue eyes, heavy dark brows, scarred face with thick lips and big white teeth. She could not imagine him any other way. He looked so perfectly *East*.

East looked up on hearing the sound of light footsteps on the stairs. His preconception was also wrong. The lady, he had guessed, would be a sixty-year-old woman altered to look like the most beautiful blond, blue-eyed, twenty-year-old goddess that ever descended from heaven, with full curves, and hair shimmering like gold. He had seen a half-dozen of those at the spaceport.

He knew she would be spoiled—one of the worthless, pampered, helpless rich. The first child born on Aeolis, her name was Laure Eva Aeolia Lorelyn Phillips DeForêt DelMar DeLaCruz Lafayette Remington.

As she descended the stairs into view, he could see that she *was* beautiful, but her hair was as dark-brown as her eyes, and she was slender, her figure more lithe and streamlined than full, more angular than the soft curved women he had seen at Oasis. And she was a genuine twenty-three; nothing looked like youth but real youth. She had high cheekbones and the thick dark lashes that every Aeolian woman had. The rest of her features were individual, especially her impish wide mouth and the spark that lived in her eyes. She looked mischievous.

East was relieved in a way. It would be easier to protect her if he did not look at her so much—not that she was hard to look at, but East rather liked the soft blondes.

Still, something should have set off danger warnings when she stopped on the stairs, her teasing mouth holding an imminent smile, and said, "You're East."

The lady was a predator herself.

"You are going to protect me?" Laure said, gliding down the remaining steps and coming to face East.

"Um hm." He nodded, looking down at her.

"You assume too much," she said, ever on the verge of smiling—or laughing. She was leading him, but he could not tell where.

East raised a quizzical eyebrow.

She clarified, "How do you presume to protect me when you cannot even find me?"

The teasing eyes held his for the briefest split second as the import of the words sank in, but before he could react—could even *think* about reacting—she was gone, wheeled and darted from view.

And she was not to be found anywhere on the estate.

On the far side of the forest there was a field white with daisies where Laure changed mounts. She jumped off her forest steed, climbed over the rail into the pasture, and sprang onto the back of a grazing palomino. She kicked with her bare heels, and it galloped away across the seemingly boundless sea of nodding white flowers.

She laughed gaily simply because she felt like it, wishing the meadow would go on forever. There was no one else in sight, no sign of her new bodyguard. The poor man never had a chance. She almost felt guilty for embarrassing him. Almost.

But as she neared the enclosing fence on the far side of the pasture, she saw with disbelief a figure leaning back against the rail, almost smiling. East.

East had been annoyed, even angry, in no mood for a game of hide and seek. But there were few things more beautiful than a running horse, and one was a running horse with a beautiful barefoot sprite astride it. East had to smile. He propped his elbows back on the rail and watched her.

The lady looked startled on seeing him, then smiled with a mouth the Aeolians called imperfect—only because they were not accustomed to wild, bright, genuine beauty. The beauty of a tiger, an eagle in flight, a woman.

East was admiring her as she brought her steed to the rail, when suddenly she asked, "Are you going to scold me?" Like an impudent child.

The illusion in his head shattered, East felt like he had been slapped. In a phrase she made him feel like her father, and he *hated* it. He was surprised at how much he hated it.

The lady was watching to see if she had struck a nerve, her eyes sharp and bright.

East was not going to give her a reaction. "I don't care what you do," he said. He avoided her eyes, looking instead at the horse, which stood quietly, not flicking its ears or swishing its tail as horses do on worlds where there are flies to be repelled.

"It's not my horse," said Laure, following his gaze. "I stole it."

If she was waiting for a reprimand, she had another thing coming. He was *not* her father. "I don't care if you steal the duchess's jewels; I'm just here to keep you from getting shot while you do it."

"You are amoral and a mercenary," she said and jumped off the horse. Her skin had a moist sheen, like dew on velvet. East was surprised to see that Aeolians sweat. Or this one did, at least.

As East helped her over the rail, she asked, "How did you find me?"

"How did you get through the forest?" East asked.

"I rode a wild horse," said Laure. "She's very shy. She's pure white and slender as a unicorn. Her hoofs are silver and cleft, she has a lion's mane, and she runs fast as the wind. You didn't answer my question."

"You didn't answer mine," said East.

"No, really, I did," she protested.

"Um hm," he grunted.

"You think I'm making this up." She was looking up at him. He was a good deal taller than she, and she had to tilt her head back to look into his sharp blue eyes. They stood there a moment, neither moving, she searching his face abused by time and sun, fascinated, not repulsed. At last something like a smile flickered across her lips, across her eyes, and she spoke. "You are going to learn to take me seriously, Mr. East."

3/8/225 *Aeolis*

Word went out to all corners of the world.

From nearby forest where Pega's horse creature carried on her back a little girl grown up who used to bring her sugar.

To northern tundra where Echo played under the frost-laced winter lights.

To the Desert of the Bells where reptiles burrowed in the singing dunes.

To the mountains that touched the heavens, where Aquilla flew her creature with Earthling birds of prey.

To the open sea where Mer's green amphibian skipped across the waves, traveling with a school of sea mammals.

To dark town lanes that Scorpii haunted as the succubus, the scorpion witch.

Word traveled on the wind to wherever the Outcast or their animals might be:

Trial.

For Draco had killed an Earthman.

3/21/225 Remington Estate,

New Africa, Southern, Aeolis

East was given a room beneath the lady's. There was no bed, for East never slept. He merely bided the long hours between dusk and dawn with the lights set at half.

When the lady appeared in the doorway, it was late and East was drunk. He was seated at the small table with several empty beer bottles, one full bottle just opened, a deck of cards, and his squashed hat. His gun was on a chair beside him under the table.

He kicked out a chair across from him for Laure, hoping he was not expected to get up and toady to her like a gentleman. In his sanctuary she could follow his rules.

She accepted the chair without comment, as if East were naturally not supposed to have any manners.

"Drink?" He raised a dark eyebrow at her.

"Yours," she said and reached across the table to snatch his beer bottle, and drank from it. She set it down on the table before her and rested her hands on either side of it, watching East like a cat with a toy between its paws, daring him to steal her prize.

East got another beer.

The lady was dressed in a flowing white kimono, and East had thought he was dreaming when she first glided into the room. It was not till she grabbed his beer that he fully realized that it was actually Laure.

In the half-light there was a sense of time suspended, as if they could step out of real time and space, and meet just once on common ground where there was no society, no rank, just the two of them in some gray world in between. It was night, and things were not quite real at this hour. East felt that if he turned up the lights, Laure would disappear.

"What brings you to the slave's quarters?" East asked in a deep voice, articulate despite the alcohol.

"I couldn't sleep," she said.

Her dark hair was still carefully done, pulled back into a mass of loose curls at the nape of her neck, a small curl in front of each ear, and one over her forehead.

*When she was good she was very very good; when she was
bad she was Laure.*

She had removed her language nodule and all her jewelry.
Without the nodule she spoke English, French, and Arabic,
could understand East's Americanese but disdained to speak
it.

The sleeves of her kimono left off at her elbows, and her
forearms looked very fragile and narrow. She pointed a slender finger at the game of solitaire laid out on the table between them. "Deal those."

"It's unlucky to have a woman at the card table," said
East, gathering up the cards to shuffle them. His eyes were
narrow slits of piercing blue.

"Why is that?"

"They invariably win."

"Then I am in no danger of gambling away my assets."

"The Remington fortune."

"No, the LaFayette fortune," she said. "I don't have much
to say in Stephen's holdings, nor he in mine."

"What do you traffic in?"

She smiled. "Don't make it sound illegal. I own a shipping
line. My great-great-great-great-great-great-great-great-great-
great-grandmother founded the first commercial interstellar
spaceline. I also own a few space stations that turn a toler-
able profit, a mining operation on Haverin-oku, and a lumber
store to keep me respectable."

"A touch of Old Guard," East said.

She smiled again. "Yes, do I look like a parvenue? I have
five kings in my ancestry, one queen, and a sovereign
princess," she said. "Oh, and one duke."

"Everyone has his poor relations," said East.

Laure laughed. "East, you're drunk," she said gleefully.

"Maybe, but not so drunk that I don't know I don't have
anything to bet against a shipping line."

"Well then, you tell me something now," she said. "I've
told you my family history. Where are you from?"

"Arizona," he said, setting the cards aside.

"What planet is that?"

"It's a state in the United States of America. Next to the
Navaho nation."

"How did you find me today?"

"A tracker," said East.

"But what did you key in on?"

"Pearls. You were wearing pearls."

Her hands went to her neck, where the fine strand had been. "So do lots of women," she said.

"Not in the middle of the forest," said East. "How did you cross the forest?"

"I told you."

"You're not playing fair."

"I never play fair," said Laure. She was looking him over intently. "Why don't you have a language nodule?"

"I do," he said, turning his head to show a small bar behind his ear.

"I'm jealous," she said. "How ever did you afford one so compact? That one is smaller than mine."

"An advantage of being a criminal," said East. "I was a guinea pig for this model."

Her eyes widened in awe. "They did *experiments* on you!"

"It wasn't so bad," said East, then smiled wryly and added, "I was one of the successes."

"Tell me what else you've done," she demanded, and she meant it. She leaned on her arm and listened to him half the night, enthralled, her eyes bright in admiration.

As East spoke he was trying to figure out why she had come. It was not for his sake, certainly—there was no pity in Laure. For her own sake, then; whether curious or lonely or simply bored, he could not tell. Beyond a point she was very hard to read. Some things were obvious. She was a spoiled, selfish, strong-willed, games-playing lady with a large streak of cruelty and a fascination with adventure. East wondered if she knew just how bloodless and sterile was the world she called hers, for she was a little too alive and too primitive for it.

That much was there for anyone to see, but subtleties she guarded more closely.

At last she sighed. "I haven't done anything." She had switched to Swiss coffee by then and was staring into the china cup. "Nothing to speak of. I didn't think anyone ever did except in books." She lifted her eyes to East. "I flew through the eye of a hurricane once. That's something I did. You always hear the expression, 'still as the eye of a hurricane,' but no one who says it has ever seen one. So I went. It was wonderful. All that roaring wind hammering at my ship—then perfect stillness surrounded by a dark wall of wind. That perfect calm in the middle of all that power." Then she giggled. "There were clouds in there. I didn't expect clouds.

"Father was furious. I was eighteen years old but he spanked me. Then *I* was furious. Mamá wouldn't have stood for that."

"Where is your mother?" East asked. He could not recall her being mentioned before.

"She died," Laure said, twisting the corner of a linen napkin. It was very late and her guard seemed to have slipped just for a short time, and the predator turned a vulnerable side to him—whether out of trust or carelessness there was no telling. "She just *died*. It was so fast. It was a brain hemorrhage. There was a tumor in there they didn't know she had. Something happened and she just died. Just like that. It shouldn't have happened. Not with all those examinations you need to enter Aeolis. If they can prevent every last germ from coming here, surely they can detect a tumor in a lady's head the size of my fist. They tell me the computer wasn't programmed to look for it. Then, dammit, what *are* they programmed for? Doctors are all charlatans."

East agreed. "My father always told me never to trust a man with an artificial brain." That eliminated all doctors who relied on medical nodules for their expertise—which left the Navaho medicine men, the only physicians East's father would consult.

"Very wise man, your father," said Laure. "After Mamá died they found a tumor in my head and took it out. I like to think Mamá gave her life for me. Otherwise it makes no sense at all."

She had been absently fingering East's hat, then she looked down at it as if seeing it for the first time. "Oh, this is awful." She pushed it away from her.

She got up, yawned sleepily, and went out, the interim at an end, reality returned. East was alone, the stillness deeper for having been broken.

In fact there was a gaping hole in it such as had never been.

3/22/225 Ledges,
New Africa, Southern, Aeolis

Leader skipped over the Ledges with the agility of a creature bred to them. It was dawn, the sun not yet appeared on the horizon, but the gray sky was lightening. Mist hung in the canyons yet, caught between the ledges and in dark corners where crickets sang. It was Leader's favorite time of day, when he took joy in just being *alive* to run, breathe, feel the air rush over him and sing in his ears, while the sun dispelled the dreaded darkness. He was always afraid the sun would not rise today, and always rejoiced when it did. It did not take much to make Leader happy.

He followed down a narrow winding fissure, deeper into the rock, the momentum carrying him in a leap over a crevasse lying on a lateral course to his path, and he ran up, out of the rock, onto the ridge, and down. He jumped, stretched his limbs, and plunged down another familiar track, around the tower—

—and ran straight into a wall that was never there before. The wall was alive, and it was Draco.

Leader staggered back in surprise, lost his footing, and fell on the rock path. He got up uneasily, Draco making no motion to help, making no motion at all, merely staring—hard. Draco did not move from Leader's path, knowing where Leader was headed—back to the Cave of the Winds to hide from the light he adored. The sun was rising now, the mist clearing, the ledges popping and cracking, expanding with the change in temperature, and already the sky was bright enough to hurt Leader's eyes.

"So you're summoning a trial," Draco said, his voice hard and smooth.

"Yes."

"Why?"

"There has been a murder," said Leader.

"Has there indeed?" Draco seemed to loom larger, his voice remaining almost musical in mockery. "What do you suppose the circle will do to me?"

"Cast you out," said Leader.

Draco seemed surprised, but then he laughed. "We shall see."

"The Ancient Ones would will it. Get out of my way," Leader said.

"You are not an Ancient One," Draco continued leisurely. "You are not even an Old One. You are not even numbered among the Young Ones. You are one of *us*."

Leader was squinting from the day's glare, impatient to be gone. "Then what are we?"

"I don't know, but we are not *them*. We—"

"*Isa*," said Leader quickly at the sound of footsteps on rock. "Someone's coming." And Leader faded back into the sheltering cliffs.

Draco, angered by the interruption that had cost him his confrontation, darted onto an overhang to peer down at the intruders—Earthlings.

There were two of them. He recognized one, a little brat of an Earth girl now a woman. Everyone treated her like some kind of native because she was born on the planet. If the dragon were to come out of the cliffs they would see she died like any other Earthling.

But the other Earthling with her carried a gun, so Draco decided to let her live. For now.

Lady Laure Remington walked among the Ledges, accompanied by her bodyguard, who looked like something salvaged. His hat was one of those which wives sneak into the disposal if they can get their hands on it. But East had no wife, and the hat, like his gun, was always with him, like a mangy, flea-bitten, old, faithful dog.

It had been two weeks since East had come to Aeolis, and he still did not know what he was protecting Laure from. He contacted the Serviceship *Halcyon XLV* to see if they could tell him something. The captain told him they had no ideas except that his old crewmate Roxanna Douglas was chasing dragons.

But then Roxanna *always* had a dragon by the tail, East recalled.

East himself did not believe in man-eating monsters, though something was definitely bizarre on this world. The Morts were coming from somewhere.

Morts. The very idea would send his Navaho aquaintances

into cold panic in their loathing of death. Father would advise him to have a care for their "superstitions." East did not believe in ghosts either, but he never turned away a Navaho blessing.

Laure danced through a wind-carved portal and struck a pose, framed in rock and sunlight.

East looked on in tolerant amusement.

"I used to run away when I was a little girl," Laure said.

"You still do," East remarked. He squinted blue eyes at the shining rocks towering over him, very much like the mesas of home, sandstone banded with gold and carmine red, some of the most beautiful country left on Earth.

Laure laughed. "When I used to run away I would come here and no one could find me. I love it. It's grand, it's wild, and it's haunted. There are ghosts all through it. And it isn't man-made. The only thing on this planet that is real."

Then she did know. She was aware of the artificiality of the world in which she lived—and she tried to escape.

Laure, I could take you from this gilded cage.

No sooner had the thought formed in East's mind than he was shocked by it. When had this happened? How had he let it?

Laure had wandered a few steps away from him, inattentive to East's change in color. His face had gone perfectly pale, then scarlet. He could have laughed if he were not so mortified. He thought with rueful mockery, *She's not even blond.*

"They tried to take into account the wind when they developed this planet," Laure was saying. "But for all their planning they could not rein the wind. It does as it pleases. They named this planet well. The wind is the one thing we cannot control—and *it* rules here."

She turned and looked at her bodyguard. Her eyes settled on his weapon. "Would you kill for me?" she asked.

"If I had to," he said.

"East, if you are so good in unarmed combat, why do you need a gun?"

"Unless you can catch bullets or ray beams with your bare hands you shouldn't face a gun unarmed."

She cocked her head. "You can't do anything against a gun without a gun?"

"I wouldn't say *that* exactly." He gave her his weapon. It

was a large, heavy projectile type. Beam guns and more so-phisticated weapons had been outlawed for their extraordi-nary ranges, which gave blunders the gravest consequences and assassins virtual impunity. "Shoot me," he said.

Not one to shy from weapons as genteel folk were gener-ally expected, Laure swung the gun onto her hip, slammed back the bolt and would have really shot him had not East been faster. He kicked the snub barrel aside, and a bullet sang into the cliffs. Startled birds rose keening, and small hoofs clattered from the ledges above. East wrested the gun from Laure before she could get off a second shot.

Instead of being cowed, Laure laughed. Her eyes gleamed with barbarian sparks. She was not a pacifist like Stephen.

"You're pretty fast for an old man," she said with a foxlike smile.

"You're pretty dirty for a lady," said East.

"*Touché*," said Laure. "But can you blame me for throw-ing you a small test? I have entrusted you with my life."

"Your husband entrusted me with your life," East correct-ed her.

Not as inattentive as she sometimes seemed, Laure had not missed anything. She used her own weapons well and her aim was deadly. "Stephen," she said pointblank, "is much too trusting."

3/23/225 *Ledges,*

New Africa, Southern, Aeolis

Evening. A Gathering.

It had taken fifteen days to find and collect all the Outcast from where they were scattered across the globe. They had come to give Draco a trial.

There was a fiery glow of sunset on the windswept Ledges, and streaks of orange and black across the twilight sky. Leader stood upon a cliff, arms outstretched to someone, any-one, to beg for guidance. No one answered.

He let his arms fall. He looked down below at the ring of twenty-three. The nameless twenty-three who were called by names that were not their own:

Draco

Leo

Lupus

Scorpii

Pega

Little Bird

Vulpi

Tauri

Aquilla

Mona

Mer

Pytho

Lepus

Basilisk

Baby

Echo

And seven nameless sisters called collectively the Pleiades, mistresses of seven white dogs.

Leader himself made twenty-four. Altogether they were the Outcast, the Creatures, the Last Ones, shunned by the Ancient Ones and the Old Ones.

It was time for Leader to begin to exercise his fragile power. As indecisive a being as was ever called Leader, his only strength was in the hope that the ring would back him up. "Draco, step center," he ordered softly from his position on the ledge.

"I should never have set you up there, Leader. I won't go," Draco protested. "I have done nothing wrong."

"The ring will decide," Leader said very quietly. "Take the center."

Draco slunk into the middle of the ring of judges and crouched there, his hands like claws in the yellow dust.

"This is the One we call Draco. His creature is a dragon," Leader announced formally. "He has caused the death of a man at his creature's doing. For this he stands trial. Draco, you may say something now."

"It was hungry," Draco said wildly. "My dragon was."

"Truth?" said Basilisk.

"Truth!" Draco barked, as if volume would diguise the lie.

The ring hissed, signaling disbelief.

"You have been called a liar, Draco," said Leader. "Someone in the ring speak."

Aquilla stood up. "Draco, you are a liar and a fool, but that is beside the point." She looked to the other members of the ring. "There has been no crime. All that was killed was a man, not one of our own. I myself will mourn the death of no Earthman. Let Draco go." ﹏

The Pleiades echoed, all seven of them, "Let Draco go."

And that ended the comments. "Do you all feel this way?" Leader asked them, squeaking out a voice that was tremulous and shrill, his eyes circling the ring below for some small sign of dissent.

"I think it is murder," said Leo.

"You don't count," said Draco.

"*Isa*, Draco, it is not your turn," Leader said. "Anyone else?"

The silence was almost a physical entity, a monster like any of their creatures, leering defeat at Leader.

"I did not realize all of you hated the Earthlings," Leader said hollowly.

"We don't. *I* don't," said Basilisk. "That does not mean we turn against one of ours for the sake of one of theirs."

"All of you feel this way?" Leader asked the circle. "An Earthling's killing is not to be called murder?"

The ring assented by silence. Lupus was sitting on Leo, pushing his face into the sand, not that one voice would help now.

Leader nearly choked. "Then, Draco, you are free to remain one of us."

"I told you this was a waste of time, Leader," said Draco up to the ledge. "I will never forget what you tried to do to me."

"Take your place in the ring," said Leader.

Draco did so.

"This gathering is at an end."

No good, no evil, no measure, just us. No Earthling was safe now, and no Outcast was safe, for there was no such thing as law, and Leader was little more than a name.

Leader wondered what the Ancient Ones thought of this breed of justice. He knew they were there, voices on a wind that did not speak to Leader.

And Leader naively assumed that they were not speaking to anyone else.

Chapter IV.
Niki

Gem Theatre, Drina Village, New Europe,
Northern, Aeolis

He sat in the balcony in a seat that had been vacant for seven years, a man of middle height, slender, slightly boyish in the face with dark eyes and brown hair. He rested his elbows on the arms of the chair, his hands folded below his chin. He was motionless, all his attention focused on the stage below, a fathomless expression on his face, completely composed and contained. His very being radiated grace, power, control, and passion, even his stillness so perfect as to be dynamic.

Niki Thea.

The dancer.

The unrivaled genius of the ballet nouveau. Within his own lifetime it was already apparent that his name would be immortal.

Mysterious and quietly temperamental, Niki Thea was given to withdrawing into his haunted mansion in the wilderness, not to be seen for years at a time, then suddenly reappearing as if he had never been gone.

He had kept himself looking as young as he had twenty years ago when he first came to Aeolis from Earth. One of the world's constants, though seasons turned and powers rose and fell, Niki never changed, an artist, a perfectionist, a scandalously egotistical innocent who in no way belonged in human society. But all he had to do was dance and he was forgiven his every transgression.

It was common knowledge that Niki Thea was mad.

His eyes followed a ballerina on the stage. She was surpassingly beautiful, her face with its prominent bones and luminous brown eyes held in holy attitude. He had to look far down the program to find her name, Mercedes Stokolska.

She betrayed no effort in her grace, her dance an incarnation of pure joy.

Then suddenly she fell.

The expression of the man in the balcony barely flinched, then was calm again, betraying nothing.

The ballerina rose, brown eyes stinging with unshed tears, and she flowed immediately back into the music. She did not hear the applause that greeted her smooth recovery. There was only the music and the dance.

She did not even notice who stood up for her.

The ballerina sat crying in her dressing room. She did not look up when footsteps stopped at her door, only at the sound of a voice she did not know as it said, "You were lovely."

She took her face from her hands and beheld him as she would an angel. Praise from Niki Thea—*the* Niki Thea—was rare as diamonds on Aeolis. And he was beautiful. To Mercedes there was nothing mortal or divine more perfect than the legend standing in her dressing-room door. She had always thought so, but this time she was not looking at a hologram. She quickly stood up, blushed. "Thank you, sir. . . . I fell."

"I saw," he said matter-of-factly. "*I* have fallen."

Mercedes braved a smile. She could not remember ever hearing of Niki Thea even missing a step, and she wondered if he just made that up to make her feel better. She was a childlike waif of a girl, twenty years old. In person she was not excessively pretty, her figure too spare, her eyes disproportionately large—a flower that closed its petals once the orchestra stopped playing.

"Your leading man sweated all over the boards," said Niki. He did not say *danseur*. That title was reserved.

Mercedes remembered her footing giving in a slick wet spot. Sweat. "That's why I fell."

"I just said that," said Niki. "You repeat me."

Mercedes was too abashed to speak. But what Niki said did not strike her as rude—Niki could say whatever he wanted.

"May I take you to dinner?" he said.

" . . . Yes . . . thank you . . ." Mercedes stammered.

"There are some friends I want to see you," said Niki.

3/23/225

Thea Estate, Wilderness, Southern, Aeolis

Who is the woman?
Niki's. She dances.
Earthling?
Pretty. Think you?
Pretty.

Niki lived on a mountain that sloped quickly down into the sea and was cleft by a river gorge so deep it looked like a crack in the world. A terrace stretched from the house to the brink of the gorge, and, over the balustrade, one could look straight *down* into the white water of the river.

Mercedes could hear the ocean very close, but could not see it for the budding trees as Niki brought her to the house.

It was spring here instead of fall, and still light, for, by the clock, they had arrived six hours earlier than they had left Drina Village.

Most of the estate was virgin forest of oak, elm, and ash, carpeted with snowy blossoms of windflowers, spring beauties, fairy lanterns, and merrybells. Violets clustered beneath the birches, bluebells grew in the canyon, zephyr lilies by the house, angel eyes in the wood fringe, and wild ginger close to the forest floor with ghostly Indian pipe and red mushrooms hiding among last season's oak leaves in the deep shade.

Mercedes had never seen a forest. She danced off the flagstone path just to be *in* it. She heard a woodpecker hammering, smelled leaves and blossoms and earth, entranced.

Niki was watching her. She turned to him, smiling nervously. "You don't know what this is like for me."

"I believe I do," said Niki. Then he turned and went inside. Mercedes skipped a few steps to catch up with him.

No servants met them inside; no one took Mercedes's shawl. There was no one about but the two of them.

A fleeting thought crossed her mind that someone with as little social *savior-faire* as Niki might decide that this was how one had his way with women, alone in a house on the edge of the wilderness. If that was his intent, she was certain there would be nothing she could do about it. He was not that much taller than she, nor was he stocky, but Mercedes sensed power, more power than in any man she had ever met.

But that did not seem to be what he had in mind, though she could not figure out what he *did* have in mind.

The house gave a homy feeling, though home was never like this. Surely crazy, it did not *feel* crazy. It was a place of varied textures and levels and no symmetry at all. The ceiling, most of it, rough-plastered, rose in levels, with wooden crossbeams supporting the most highly vaulted sections, while other parts slanted off at a steep rake. A free-standing staircase wound up out of the central room at a low gradient, taking half the length of the house to reach to a second level. And the whole place was crowded with strange clutter and furniture—like a grandmother's attic, although all the things Mercedes found were unlike anything she had ever seen.

"Where did you get all this?" Mercedes marveled, venturing into Niki's house with timid steps.

"I had it made," said Niki, watching her.

"You designed it all?"

"Not I. It is not really my house—I did not build it for myself, anyway. It is for the spirits. They tell me what they want and I have it made for them."

Raving.

At least his madness was the benign sort to create such warmth in design. The house had a comfortable atmosphere. Though odd, it was *familiar* and hospitable. The walls were friendly, crazy as they were.

The only thing that disturbed Mercedes was an occasional cross draft—from the weirdly placed windows, she guessed. "Breezy," she said.

A gust of wind at her back made her jump, and she spun to face Niki in alarm. This was *strange*.

"It *is* haunted," Niki reminded her. "If by that you mean inhabited by spirits."

Then he stopped, became very still, his attention drawn inward as a breeze from nowhere ruffled his smooth hair. "What?" he said. His brows drew together the slightest breath and he shook his head. "No," he answered an unspoken question.

Please don't be crazy, Mercedes nearly blurted out.

His eyes cleared and he was looking once again at her, offering no comment, apology, or explanation whatsoever.

He led her into the dining room, where there was still no sign of human servants, the food appearing from within the center of the table. Mecredes could not eat. It might as well have been kelp instead of real meat. She was too nervous to taste it.

If Niki noticed her distress, he did not comment on it. He seemed unaware of her, listening instead to a conversation she could not hear.

Mercedes was aware of deep silence. *God in heaven, am I being shown off to a house full of ghosts?*

The table swallowed up her cold meal and brought out a fresh one. She did not want it.

Suddenly realizing that Niki would not know Rude if it came to dinner, she got up from the table without a word and went out on the terrace.

The evening was cool, and she was glad she still had her shawl.

She leaned on the balustrade, catching her scattered thoughts. They all had to do with Niki.

She was not sure why she liked him. His silence unnerved her. She knew only too well how *she* felt, but Niki was an enigma. Soft-spoken, arrogant, obsessed with his art, with no social instinct whatever—and this was the man she let herself become attached to. The situation was totally impossible. It was just as well she was leaving Aeolis with her company in the morning—Drina Village time. It would not be long now. And she would carry home with her a story of how Niki Thea picked her up after she fell and told her she was lovely. A nice story and quite enough.

Then why did her pulse jump when he stepped out on the terrace? *I might as well be twelve years old.*

He was regarding her now with one of his unreadable expressions, his lips slightly parted, seeming very young, or very old. His eyes were . . . sad?

Mercedes dared ask, "What are you thinking?" He was, after all, thinking it while looking at *her* very intently.

"You are only here for a moment." The expression *was* sad. "Ephemeral as the mayfly."

Did he mean her stay on Aeolis?

Or her life?

"I was away for a while," he said and paused.

A while? Seven years! Where did he go? Here? A sanitarium?

"They said there was a woman I must see," he continued.

They? His ghosts?

"I did not believe them. Prima donnas come, prima donnas go. None of them dance. This time they were right."

Mercedes felt tears welling in her eyes, and she turned her face upward to keep from shedding any. She gazed up at the blurred and misty stars, far off and serene, fiery, constant, ancient. Beautiful dancers. *Ever fall in love with someone whom you had absolutely no business falling in love with?*

Niki was still looking at her, his dark eyes fixed with a look of innocence that was, at the same time, so knowing as to approach omniscience. "You are crying, Mercedes."

"No, I'm not." She looked at him and sniffed. Her eyes were watery, but there were no tears on her face.

"They say you are." He motioned with his head as if someone were standing behind him, but no one was.

He turned and spoke a few words in a language Mercedes did not recognize to someone who was not there.

Mercedes was not wearing a language nodule, for Niki spoke German as well as she, so she had no idea what he said until he shifted back to German. It upset her. A few tears rolled down her cheeks.

Niki turned back to her. "You *are* crying," he said, puzzled.

"*I know I am!*" she snapped.

"Why?"

"Nothing. I'm leaving tomorrow."

"No, you are not," he said like irrefutable fact.

It so shocked Mercedes that her tears stopped instantly. "I beg your pardon," she said, a little affronted, a little afraid.

"Quit your company," he said.

"*What!* Why?" She was ready to run, ready to scream for all the good it would do.

But Niki's face had gone from innocent arrogance to almost panic in its urgency, and when he spoke his voice had lost all authority and was plaintive. He said, "Dance for me?"

3/29/225

Gem Theatre, Drina Village, New Europe, Northern, Aeolis

Niki was beautiful in motion. Powerful, vulnerable, he loved the dance, was *in* love with it. He could mesmerize, could hold an audience on his fingertips. His own cast could not help but be swept in with his emotion when he danced, and it was wonderful just to be in his company.

But every one of his dancers dreaded when his "spirits" came to talk to him, because the spirits told him to make a change in the choreography.

Niki's eyes would focus on midair and he would begin a soliloquy. "What? . . . Does not. . . . Very well, I shall change it."

That was when he chose to speak in a recognizable language and not something that sounded like tongues.

The soliloquy was always followed by a change in the dance, and finally a question directed to the other half of his split personality: "Happy?"

Except that there finally came a time when Niki himself became upset with his spirits and decided to argue with them.

Mercedes winced, watching her love go mad. The rest of the troupe was so spellbound that they could not even giggle as Niki steadily grew more angry and at last shouted to thin air, in English this time, "If you know so much, why is it that I am here dancing and you are *nothing!*" Then immediately he blanched pale as death, and, with a cry in his voice, he recanted, "I'm sorry. I'm sorry." And he fled the stage like one possessed.

After a stunned instant, Mercedes ran after him. She darted through the stage door and came to a halt, confronted by two sets of stairs, one rising, one descending, a narrow hall winding in both directions, and a door to the outside. She picked a course at random and weaved through the backstage labyrinth, through storage rooms above the theater house, and at last passed through an arch onto a stair from which she looked down and saw Niki at the bottom of the flight. He had not fallen, but he was kneeling there, his face in his hands. A shaft of patterned gold light through a rosette window fell across the steps between them.

He did not look up, was not even aware that she was there.

Mercedes withdrew as quietly as she had come and never mentioned what she had seen, which was nothing, or what she had *felt*, which was the presence of something *there*. Something Ancient.

Chapter V.
Morts

3/29/225

Desert of the Bells, Northern, Aeolis

The Ancient One finally came to rest, weary. He had had
enough. He did not want to see his people end.
Feet touched burning sand.
Felt wonderful.
Felt.
Collapsed. Aged legs buckled. Fell heavily, face first in the
sand.
Biting heat in nostrils, in throat.
Beating sun. Skin prickled.
Pain in chest.
It was over quickly.

The robots found the body, could not identify it, collected
it and brought it to the police.
It had no ID. Another one. There seemed no end.
It was put in the trasher.
They called it a Mort.

4/1/225 *Oasis Port,*

Desert of the Bells, Northern, Aeolis

The main concourse of Oasis Port was an open-air boule-
vard of red brick flanked by palm trees. The temperature
here was several degrees cooler than the surrounding desert,
and it was a comfortable place for the three officers of the
Serviceship *Halcyon XLV* to sit and consult with Oasis's

chief of police, Luis Del Fuego, a tall handsome caballero who bowed to Captain Safir and kissed commander Douglas's hand.

The *Halcyon* had been on the planet for one Aeolian month, chasing information and floundering in red tape and hysterical stories. Finally the crew had found someone in authority who would talk to them.

Del Fuego stood at the crew's table, his foot up on a chair seat, his forearm leaning across his knee, a riding crop in his gloved hand.

Per explained how they would proceed with the investigation. "Since we can't follow up all the strange stories we've been told, we'll concentrate on the Morts. They are our one certainty—"

"Can't we look for the succubus?" Buddy interrupted. "She sounds like more fun."

"Shut up, Buddy, I'm being serious," said Per. "The succubus is just a lot of wind, like the rest of the ghost and monster stories. We'll forget the phantoms and chase down the dead bodies instead. Let's hope that when we solve that problem, the rest of the problems will solve themselves."

"If you don't mind," said Roxanna. "I would like to hear some more monster stories." She was leaning back in her wrought-iron chair, her thumbs hooked in the pockets of her tartan vest.

"Oh yes." Per grinned up at Del Fuego and winked a green eye. "Our Roxanna's jeep connected with a dragon."

"I see." Del Fuego winked back.

Roxanna drummed her fingers against her waist, agitated, not speaking.

Per snapped open a world map the police chief had given him. It was a classified document, not to be found in normal computer records. It was covered with dots, each dot representing a place where a Mort had been found.

There were at least twelve thousand dots.

Per whistled through his teeth. The residents of Aeolis were under the impression that there had been only fifteen Morts—and even that had been enough to cause alarm.

Per cleared his throat. "Let's consider this logically. What we have are several thousand unidentified . . . dead persons." He cleared his throat again. "The question is, where are they coming from? There are three possibilities that I can see.

One: They were here before Aeolis was settled. Two: They are immigrating under our noses. Three: They were born here."

"That's very logical, captain," said Roxanna. "Except that all three possibilities are impossible."

"Right. Now why are they impossible? Number one is impossible because the planet was scanned by the discovery ships for organic matter and came up negative."

"Also, may I add, *capitán*," Del Fuego interjected, "before anyone even set foot on Aeolis the world was shot through with a steray—just in case something was missed."

"Aren't sterays illegal?" Roxanna asked.

"Not two hundred and twenty-five years ago, señorita," said Del Fuego.

"So much for possibility one." Buddy shrugged.

"Possibility two," Per continued, "is prevented by the screening station on Kushuh. You can't get an unauthorized molecule through there."

"What if someone bypassed Kushuh?" Buddy suggested.

Del Fuego shook his head. "First he would have to get through the horizon guard. Then there is a force field encompassing Aeolis. A ground controller must make a window for any ship or any thing to enter or leave."

"A force field around a *whole world?*" Roxanna said.

"*Sí.*"

"That would cost a living fortune," she said.

"There is a fortune beyond imagining on Aeolis, Señorita Douglas," Del Fuego affirmed.

"That leaves possibility three," said Per. "They were born here."

But Del Fuego was shaking his head.

"What now?" Roxanna said.

"In the census scans it is true we detect some extras. We always assumed they were people we thought had left the planet but actually had not—our exits are not as controlled as our entrances. But even if these extras *are* our Morts still alive, they are not nearly enough to account for fifty or so Morts per year. The Morts must be coming in from outside."

"They must be, but they can't," Per growled.

"That is correct, *capitán*."

"How long has this been going on?" Buddy asked. "The Morts, I mean."

"Ever since there was Aeolis," said Del Fuego. "Almost two hundred and twenty-five years."

"Why wasn't the Service called in earlier?" Per asked.

"There was no reason to call." The caballero shrugged, pushing his broad-brimmed hat off his head. It hung on his back from a black braid tied at his throat. "The Morts harmed no one until one was discovered by a resident. Then the panic began. We did an excellent job of keeping them secret before then. You can see they appear in isolated areas." He gestured at the map with his riding crop. "They are usually found by the robot monitors that patrol those areas. A robot picks them up and brings them to the police because it does not know what else to do with them."

"And what do you do with them?" Per asked, already suspecting the answer.

"Dispose of them."

"Annihilate?"

"*Sí.*"

"Are they Earthling?" Per asked, using the word to mean *Homo sapiens*, not necessarily Earthborn.

"They look like Earthlings," said Del Fuego.

"You don't *know?*" All three officers started at once.

"No."

"Then they could be anything," said Per.

"It is possible they are not Earthlings," said Del Fuego.

"Has there been no autopsy?" Buddy asked.

"For what? It is obvious they died of old age. There are no facilities here, and why should we export the Morts to a clinic to find out what we already know?"

"You don't know if they are Earthlings," Per reminded him with tried patience.

"They are dead. It is all one." Del Fuego shrugged. "Must you know what they are to get rid of them?"

"You said the Morts weren't hurting anyone," said Roxanna. "But what about *them?*"

"Señorita, they aren't anyone. According to the UBC they do not even exist."

"The UBC says a human being—or at least a human*oid*—doesn't exist, so he doesn't," said Roxanna.

"Put it out of your mind, sweet señorita. You are too tender-hearted. Too much idealism will book you passage on the next ship to the Outer Reaches. We are here for the comfort of the residents. *Es todo*. That is all."

"The first thing we need," said Per, shutting the map, "is an autopsy. Del Fuego, save the next body for us."

"I will do this for you, *capitán*," said the caballero. "But please remember what I told you. You are here for the residents, not the Morts, whoever they may be. I will give you some advice. Whatever you discover, make sure it is good for the residents."

"You mean cover up anything else," Roxanna rephrased.

"I mean, señorita, you seem to enjoy breathing as much as I do. *Comprende*?"

Roxanne nodded. "I understand."

She understood that there was a fortune here beyond imagining, and she understood that there was more to this assignment than she was being told.

4/1/225

Babylon, Little Asia, Northern, Aeolis

Laure still impressed East as a cat with a toy between its paws, but now *he* was the toy. Ever since she had seen through him at the Ledges, he was totally at her mercy, and it was quite obvious that she had none.

He had never met anyone who could make him so angry, but he could not find it within himself to hate her. Anger he could find, but no hatred.

It was a possession game. She made it clear that she was not for the likes of him, but neither would she let him off her string. It pleased her to have power over him enough to hurt him. Lest he forget, she would drive in her goad to watch him wince and make sure she still had him.

And still he could not hate her.

Trust she granted him, but not the kind that is a gift. Rather it was trust as a matador turning his back on a bull trusts the beast not to charge because both know well who is master.

Either way, Laure showed East the Aeolis few people ever saw, and, in this, East was taken into the lady's confidence as he was certain her husband had never been.

East had seen pitbull fights, and he had seen the poor

man's version of it, cockfighting, so he should not have been surprised by Aeolis's version of the sport. In fact, he should have expected it.

The cellar of the restaurant, where Laure had led him past a security system worthy of a bank, looked like a speakeasy except that drinking was not what was illegal here. Sunk in the center of it was a large pit. In the pit were gladiators.

East knew better than to register shock. He felt Laure's eyes on him, waiting for his reaction. He turned to her. Her face was filled with anticipation—like a willful child, laughter in the corners of her eyes and lips, wondering if she was to be spanked, daring him to.

He did not change expression while he regained his balance.

Of course there was nothing to be done, not by him, and not by her. There was simply too much wealth, too much power, here. Laure was merely showing off a guilty secret, making him feel more like her father—making him more exasperated and angry with her. That disturbed him more than what was going on in the pit. He had long since ceased to be shocked by murder, even for bored sport.

The lady was waiting. He said simply, "Are you going to place a bet?"

Her eyes widened very slightly and her mouth lost its upward tilt, dissolving into amazement. "No proper expression of horror, Mr. East?"

"I'm not your father." That was hardly the point, and he realized it once he had said it. He regretted letting it slip, but it had been coming a long time.

"But don't you disapprove of what is being done here?" she said. That she had caught the irrelevance of his reply was evident from the teasing lilt in her voice.

East attempted to salvage the situation. "What point is there in disapproving when there is nothing to be done?"

"I'm so glad you see that," she said. "No. No, I'm not. I wanted to argue with you about it."

She walked over to the pit. She made no bet, but her face took on a glow of excitement as the fighting became intense.

The fight was not elaborate, little better than a bloody wrestling match between naked contestants using ineffective weapons, which only emphasized the luridness and illegality. That, East supposed, was the charm of it for these overrefined aristocrats. Still, it seemed a strange thing to find on a world where bullfights and boxing were outlawed as cruel, and gentlefolk became nauseated at the sight of a scratch or a scab.

Some of the spectators had been transformed into orgiastic, salivating, rolling-eyed fanatics. Laure betrayed her feral spark, yet, if taken out of her present surroundings, she would still look the lady.

But East knew where she was, knew what caused the flush in her cheeks. It did not repel him. The primitive had always lurked very close to the surface of the lady. Perhaps that was what had attracted him in the first place.

He glanced down into the pit, dispassionate, thinking that one of the two combatants would die, and he thought of Morts. At the same moment as he made the connection he realized that it was wrong. This could not be the source of the Morts. Morts were aged and unwounded and unidentified. This was not a place where unknown people mysteriously appeared; it was where known ones disappeared, for good. Their deaths would be easy enough to cover by saying that the people in question left the planet. Exits from Aeolis were considerably less regulated than entrances, and it would be a simple matter to explain the disappearance of a commoner as an undetected exit.

Gladiators, Morts, dragons, ghosts. It was hard to say what related to what. East shook his head. That problem was for the crew of the *Halcyon* to figure out. And if the Service was to find out about the gladiators, it would not be from him. It was not what he was being paid for.

East leaned over Laure's shoulder and, watching her watching the two men in the pit as they tore, bled, and staggered, he asked in a whisper, "Are they volunteers?"

Laure turned her head to him. "Only sometimes."

4/4/225

Lake Simkhah, Little Asia, Northern, Aeolis

Aeolis was an old world, older than Earth, orbiting a slow-burning sun that was older than Sol and would outlast Sol. And like all old worlds, Aeolis guarded its ancient

secrets, secrets deeper than Earthlings relieving their boredom
with their own kind's bloodshed in sordid little hideaways.

In some ways the planet had not been thoroughly probed
and scanned, despite the care that had gone into its develop-
ment. Its inner makeup had been plumbed enough to ensure
that it was geologically quiet; quakes were few and of little
consequence, for areas around major faults had been left as
wilderness regions. There had also been scans for organic
matter and for unnatural radiation, both of which came up
negative. These were specific scans searching for something in
particular. Because they gave insufficient evidence of life on
Aeolis, no archaeological scan had been done.

An archaeological scan was a general, limited-depth scan,
extremely costly because it was searching for nothing definite,
and so recorded *everything*.

Commander Roxanna Douglas put in a request for an archaeological scan. Everyone, even Roxanna, was surprised
when the Service granted it, for she had given no proposed
site, no expectations for finds, and no reason for the request.

Roxanna was a very methodical archaeologist. To pick a
site to scan, she tacked up a map of the world over Per's dartboard, closed her eyes, and tossed a dart. It landed in a lake,
so she decided to scan the lake's perimeter.

After the three days it took to clear Kushuh, a fully
equipped survey ship and crew was at Roxanna's disposal.
She took it out to the shores of Lake Simkhah and sank a
probe beam to bedrock level, and got a sounding almost immediately.

"Anomaly, commander," said the ship's reader.

"What is it?" said Roxanna.

"Aluminum."

"That's as common as bars on Kushuh," said Roxanna.

"*Metallic* aluminum isn't," said the reader. "It's an alloy,
ninety-four percent aluminum, four percent copper, point
seven percent manganese, point eight percent magnesium."

"Could it be something somebody buried? How deep is it?"

"It's fifteen meters down. I don't interpret the data, ma'am.
Do you want a picture of it?"

The scanner was ringing more anomalies, one after another.

"Yes," said Roxanna.

The reader turned on the screen, on which the computer

put a scaled-down drawing of the aluminum object. "Take a look," said the reader.

Roxanna stared at it. "I don't believe it."

4/4/225 *Oasis Port,*

Desert of the Bells, Northern, Aeolis

"It's an airplane," Per said.

It was not of any Earth design from any era, but there was no mistaking what it was the computer had drawn.

Per scowled over the printout Roxanna had given him.

"There's a whole field of them down there," said Roxanna. "Ninety of them. And don't tell anyone, but I stole something from the find site."

She pulled out of her jacket pocket a little figurine of a horselike creature, but its hoofs were cleft, its mane covered its entire neck, and it was not as stocky as a horse. "There were dozens of these. I didn't think it would be missed."

Per sneered at it. "Looks like something you picked up in a souvenir shop."

Roxanna blanked, then said slowly, "It just might be. It was in a building by the airfield filled with all sorts of junk like this. Except the 'souvenir shop' is ten thousand years old—give or take two thousand years."

Per was silent. Buddy picked up the horse figure. "You'll never make an archaeologist, Rox. The first rule of archaeology is that everything you find has to be religious. Take this. It's obviously a votive object and the room that contained them all by the airport was obviously a travelers' shrine—"

"Buddy, do you want to wake up some morning to find your dimples filled in with quick plastic?" Roxanna snatched her horse back.

Per was scowling. "Why the hell did you dig up *that* and not the airfield?"

"There's a mosque," said Roxanna.

"There's always a mosque," said Buddy before Roxanna could elbow him to shut up.

"I'd like to see the airplanes myself," Roxanna told Per. "As near as we can tell without digging them up they're also about ten thousand years old, but they're all imcomplete. Any fittings that would have been made of plastic or rubber or steel if it were an Earth plane just aren't there or somehow fell apart. In fact, anything that had carbon in it *doesn't* anymore. Do you know there are no diamonds on Aeolis? Do you know there wasn't any CO_2 here? They had to *pump* it into the atmosphere—a whole worldful—before they could grow anything. All the natural carbon on Aeolis is free. There are no naturally occurring carbon compounds, but it looks as if there used to be some. It's as if the carbon just fell out of everything. It's really bizarre."

"Well," said Per, "now that you have managed to make yourself famous and got your name in the news, do you think you can settle down and stop playing captain?"

Roxanna blinked, blinked twice, bewildered. "Per, I—"

"There have always been too many captains on board this ship, commander," Per continued.

"Sir, I didn't—"

"And while you are at it, tell me, what has any of this to do with the Morts? What has it got to do with anything we're try to do?"

Roxanna could not speak for a moment. *Why is he doing this to me?* "I . . . I don't know—yet."

"Have you forgotten our assignment? But then you never could follow orders."

"It does tie in," said Roxanna, stepping back from him, hugging her little horse figurine. *He has no right to shoot me down like this. He has no right.*

"How?" said Per.

"I don't know. But it does. Sir."

Somehow.

4/14/225

Cape Heartbreak, Polaris, Aeolis

"Captain! We finally got one!" Roxanna cried into the radio built into her heated suit. She brushed ice crystals from her visor and adjusted her light. All around her, powdery snow shifted with a swirling arctic wind, while overhead, eerie curtains of colors were dancing in the sky. It was noon, but the sun never rose above the horizon during winter on the arctic island Polaris.

"One what?" Per's sullen and impatient voice answered

over the radio. In the background, Roxanna could hear the sound of darts stabbing into a board.

"A Mort," she answered. "It's the same as all the others were described: naked, old, no record of ever coming to Aeolis, no identity in the known galaxy, no evidence of how he even got to Polaris. Looks like he died of old age—either that or froze to death. But I couldn't tell you whether he was an Earthling or some other kind of humanoid."

The darts stopped. Per's voice came over the radio, "Okay, bring him in. We'll have him shipped out for an autopsy right away."

Roxanna signed off and walked back to the police transport that had brought her here.

Now we'll see if we're dealing with Earthlings or what.

4/14/225 *Remington Estate,*
New Africa, Southern, Aeolis

It was still early evening at the Remington Estate. Laure was curled up in an armchair by the fire, which East had built for her, warming herself and feeling snug. She had been caught in an unscheduled rain that afternoon, but was now dry and pretty again, no worse for the drenching. Her dark hair was uncurled, newly dry and brushed, and full of static. Electric wispy tresses fell on her shoulders and across her brow.

East stood by her chair, holding his hat out to the heat, for Laure had refused to let the servants put it in the dryer with the rest of their wet clothes. Laure had tried to throw it in the fire, but East grabbed it from her and warned her very firmly not to try it again.

"Yes, Daddy," she shot at him.

The remark hit home and hurt, as it was supposed to. Worse.

No matter how many times he worked it out, three times twenty-three was sixty-nine. He was seventy. That was nearly half a lifetime. Why shouldn't she treat him like her father—or her grandfather?

When I am in my twilight years, you will be as old as I am now.

He would have laughed at the absurdity of the situation, but he felt too deeply to laugh. Why in the name of merciful God *this* woman? It was bad enough that she owned him, but did she have to *know* it?

The man East least wanted to see—or even acknowledge

the existence of—chose this moment to appear. Laure's husband.

Stephen Remington's manner of entering a room was almost an apology, as if he needed permission to move about in his own house.

"Laure, darling," said the vanilla man, unaware that he was interrupting a duel and that East was staggering from a well-aimed dart fired by sweetly Cheshire-smiling Laure.

Can't he see the blood all over the carpet?

Laure could see it. She missed nothing.

"My darling," Stephen began again. "You . . . I . . ."

"Yes, darling?" Laure prompted.

"Dr. Dittrich was here yesterday. . . . "

"I know that," Laure said. The bothersome doctor had insisted on checking her over—of course she knew he had been there.

"I'm afraid you have cancer."

East nearly choked. Laure was perturbed. "How can I?" she said. "I thought there were no diseases on this planet."

"It is not a germ, Laure. You don't *catch* it."

"Then, darling, how come I *have* it?" said Laure sweetly.

"I don't know how these things work. But you must go to the Yrlin clinic right away."

"I must?" said Laure, beginning to show real annoyance, unused to hearing orders, especially from Stephen.

"Dr. Dittrich said it was quite extensive," Stephen said.

"Herr Dittrich is a quack. They all are."

"Darling," said Stephen, "doesn't it hurt?"

"What of it?" Laure's eyes flashed in betrayal. She should never have told a doctor what she did not want the whole galaxy to know. She was angry that her secret had been discovered, and furious that it had been broadcast.

East was astounded. *Dammit, the woman's been in pain!* And he had never noticed. It was something she kept very close to her in her headstrong foolish way.

Though gut reaction said go to her, East recognized it was time for fading into the background, and he stepped back so that he was no longer between the lord and the lady.

"Laure, please," said Stephen. "Just four days and you will be as good as new. It is a painless procedure, the doctor assured me."

Laure's face was sweetly serene, but East had learned to

read her eyes, and her eyes were sneering with contempt at the offer of painlessness as if it were something that should matter to her. It did not carry the weight with her that it did with Stephen.

"And they have perfected it so you never have to go back."

"They had *better* have perfected it," said Laure.

"Laure, it's for your health," Stephen begged.

"Very well," she consented. "I shall go for you." Then she spoke past her husband to her bodyguard. "East, what do you think of doctors?"

"Not much," said East without expression, his face an impassive mask.

"There, you see, darling? East agrees with me."

Stephen turned to face the hired man. "Mr. East, there are pressing matters I have to attend to. With the reentry procedures, I'm afraid I won't be able to accompany Mrs. Remington to the clinic. I know it is not exactly in the contract, but would you mind so very much looking after her? I hate to see her travel off-planet, and I forbid her to go alone." The word *forbid* did not sound convincing coming from Stephen. "I will, of course, adjust your salary accordingly."

East did not trust himself to speak. *What exactly do you call a pressing matter?* He merely nodded.

"Oh, good." Laure danced over and hugged East's arm. "Maybe we shan't go to the clinic at all. You could take me to see something else."

East turned to the lady on his arm. "I'm hired to take you to the clinic."

"You are a mercenary," she said lightly, but she did not sound convinced. She could see through his every facade, and at this point he was almost glad, for there was a hint of fear in her dark eyes, and she was holding his arm much tighter than in play. She was too proud to let herself admit she might fall, but he was there to catch her if she did. She might never thank him, never express it, even deny it, but to be needed by this woman just this once was enough for East.

4/16/225 Oasis Port,

Desert of the Bells, Northern, Aeolis

The three crewmembers of *Halcyon XLV* grew impatient waiting for the autopsy report on their Mort, and when finally it was prepared, the Service would not give it to them. They were told that it did not make sense and it was classified.

"Hell of a way to run an investigation," Per growled.

"What is so classified about a dead body?" Buddy asked. Then they began to think about the possibilities, and all three stopped talking, stopped breathing for a moment, overcome by the feeling that the Service had sent them up a very tall ladder and suddenly snatched it out from under them.

Buddy suddenly spoke again, too loudly, too cheerfully. "Don't look so morbid; after all, we're talking about a Service that once arrested a bologna sandwich for espionage."

The sandwich really had been arrested. Someone had mistaken "bologna sandwich" for a code name and reacted accordingly when said bologna sandwich was reported to be in a red-card room overnight. When apprehended at gunpoint, the offending sandwich was denied its rights and promptly fed to a police dog.

"It's probably just another administrative blunder," said Buddy. "Why else would they withhold information from the crew that is investigating the problem for them?"

There was a pause.

"I have to know," said Roxanna.

"I do too," Buddy admitted.

Per spoke slowly. "Then let's hope it is easier to smuggle something *out* of Aeolis than *into* Aeolis."

"A dead body?" Roxanna said skeptically.

If it were a secret autopsy he was suggesting, there was another Mort available, being held in a funeral parlor's preservation tank. But smuggling it from the parlor and shipping it off-planet without attracting attention did not seem feasible.

"Not the whole Mort," Per corrected Roxanna. "A biopsy of one. It won't tell us everything, but at least we'll know if we've got an Earthling or one of our humanoid allies or someone else."

"How is a biopsy going to be any easier to smuggle out than a whole Mort?" said Roxanna. "The Service will still get suspicious if the *Halcyon* suddenly leaves Aeolis and heads for a clinic."

"That's true, but the *Halcyon* does not have to leave. I happen to know someone headed to a destination we want our biopsy to go. You might know him, Roxanna. He's an old crewmate of yours."

Roxanna rolled her eyes before he even finished, knowing who he was going to name. *Not him.*

"Remember East?"

Aeolian date 4/18/225

Yrlin Clinic, Bhaccaa

Laure took over the clinic. Her room, her suite, was quickly decorated to look like no hospital room East had ever seen—except for the flowers.

"It looks like a Chsenian wake," said East of the hundreds of flowers in elaborate arrangements, most of them sent by Stephen. East had given her two roses in a beer bottle, which she kept beside her at the head of the bed on a nightstand.

East looked at her and thought of the soft blondes at the spaceport. They paled by comparison. This woman had ruined him for life.

"Why did you leave me alone?" she pouted, sitting up in bed, leaning back on a satin-covered pillow, her dark hair loose, brushed and rebrushed out of boredom.

East had left Laure soon after they had arrived at the clinic in order to find a research physician who would analyze the contents of a freezer capsule he had smuggled out of Aeolis for the crew of the *Halcyon XLV*. He was aware that the biopsy was of extreme importance, for nothing else would have induced Roxanna Douglas to talk to him again, much less ask him for help. But East had told Laure nothing regarding that. The matter was secret. So he avoided the question and excused his absence. "You are perfectly safe here."

"Perfectly miserable," said Laure. "I shall die of boredom if I stay here another minute."

"You will die of cancer if you don't," said East. He

glanced at his chronometer. It was time to meet the research physician to get the report.

The motion did not escape Laure. "Stay with me," she said.

"I have something to take care of," said East.

Laure put her brush down in her lap. "You are supposed to be taking care of *me*."

East stepped out the door. "I'll be back."

Aeolian date 4/18/225

Yrlin Clinic, Bhaccaa

The research physician was a small brown alien with whiteless black eyes, no hair, six fingers on each hand, seven prehensile toes on each foot, a gargling voice, and vaguely masculine body. He loved to analyze. The first thing he said to East, after a critical look, was, "You drink too much."

"I don't need a doctor to tell me that," said East. "Tell me about the biopsy."

A long, skinny-fingered hand squeezed East's arm. "Good muscle tone."

East snatched his arm out of the Bhaccaan doctor's grasp and growled, "The biopsy."

The physician held up a plastic card on which was recorded in micropattern the results of the analysis of the Mort biopsy. "Is this a joke?" the alien gargled.

"Why?" said East.

"I should be able to reconstruct the entire organism from what you gave me, but I cannot. Did someone fabricate this just to fool me?"

"Just tell me what you found," said East. "Is it an Earthling?"

"No. It is not anything. Each cell—each and every cell— has one and a half sets of chromosomes. The complete set is humanoid, the half-set is a rather ingeniously conceived mammalian, and there is some other unidentifiable *stuff* in there that serves no purpose that I can tell. It's very clever, but if someone expects me to believe that is an alien life form you gave me, tell him I am not convinced. I can recognize interference with nature when I see it, and I tell you someone *made* that."

Chapter VII.
The Ghosts of Aeolis

Aeolian date 4/18/225

Yrlin Clinic, Bhaccaa

Laure had fled her flower-laden hospital suite, and she stood outside in the misty gray drizzle on the balcony that opened at the end of her hall. All the trees were bare, and the season here could have been spring or autumn, or even winter for all she knew.

She sensed without turning that she was no longer alone. She knew who had stepped out on the balcony with her. She knew his step, knew his smell, knew the way his presence felt. She did not have to look, and her present stance lent her greater authority.

East leaned on the doorframe, a micropattern card and a piece of man-made somebody in a freezer capsule in his pocket. He had an urge to pitch both over the balcony, forget the Service, forget Stephen Remington, take Laure by the hand, and go away as far as her ship *Windhover* would take them.

But would Laure go?

Despite everything that East considered wrong with Lord Stephen Remington, Laure remained steadfastly faithful to her husband. And her damned loyalty was one of the things that made her attractive.

Did she know that too?

East's father would have a solution to this situation. East could almost hear him giving advice on how to handle Stephen: "Shoot 'im!"

But East could not be certain the lady would forgive him

for exterminating her bland pet. The bitter reality remained whatever he did: Laure loved Stephen.

East regarded her slender figure on the balcony, her back turned to him, her hair limp from the dampness.

I love you, woman. It was not even pure lust, and that surprised and frustrated him. Why her? East had previously considered God to be a fair man.

"Laure, where is my hat?" said East.

"I threw it out," she said without turning.

East stepped beside her at the rail with deadly glare. "You what?"

"It was dreadful. Besides, I'm very angry with you."

East started to speak, but floundered in exasperation.

Laure turned to him. She was very white, her eyes smoky. She tightly gripped the edges of her shawl, her narrow arms crossed defensively. "Don't you *ever* leave me alone like that again."

"I won't," said East.

"*Ever.*" She was not going to cry. She already had.

East wanted to touch her but did not dare. He could only answer, "As long as you say."

4/20/225 *Kushuh*

East had come as far as Kushuh with the illegal biopsy analysis card when he realized the impossibility of smuggling it down to the planet surface. Were he to try, the card would be seized, scanned, recognized by the UBC as classified, and East would be arrested on the spot. So, since he could not bring the card down to the *Halcyon*, he summoned *Halcyon*'s crew up to Kushuh.

Per Safir started out immediately and told Buddy and Roxanna to draw straws to see who accompanied Per to Kushuh and who stayed behind aboard the *Halcyon* to throw smoke screens over the activities of the other two. Roxanna pulled the short straw, but, outranking Buddy, she ordered him to break his. Pouting, Buddy held up a shorter straw. Roxanna patted his shoulder, "Bad luck, mate." She grabbed her jacket and ran to catch up with Per on his way to the Kushuh shuttle bay.

Twenty minutes later the two officers walked into the place

of rendezvous. Roxanna stopped dead inside the door and muttered, "I can guess who picked this dive."

It was a tavern, the lights turned down so low she could barely see that the walls had been scored by beam-gun burns and the tabletops slashed with bayonets.

The place was almost deserted. Per and Roxanna joined East at a table along one wall.

Per was disturbed by the presence of Lady Laure Remington. She had insisted on being included in East's conspiracy, and there was no saying no to her.

Roxanna derived sadistic pleasure in the lady's being there. The Servicewoman could see in a moment that the spoiled aristocrat had East wrapped tightly around her finger. Those two deserved each other. Roxanna only regretted that she could not fully enjoy her gloat, for she had more pressing things on her mind.

Finally in possession of the information the Service had withheld from them, the officers now knew less than before, and they sank into a taut silence. The only one who seemed unconcerned was Laure, who stirred her drink with an obscene swizzle stick and looked around the tavern with curiosity, straining to overhear a conversation at the bar where two off-duty customs officers, sky-high on seized contraband, were asking the barkeep if he knew anyone who wanted to bid on a pitbull they were holding in quarantine. Laure was immune to the uneasiness of her company. If she sensed danger at all, it did not frighten her.

Roxanna drummed her fingers on the table until Per slapped her hand to make her quit, then she said, "What about natives?" Her voice was barely above a whisper. "*Returning* natives. Someone built those airplanes ten thousand years ago. Where are they now? What if Aeolians ten thousand years more advanced than we are have found a way through our screens and jammers and are returning to claim their planet?" She glanced at her captain for a reaction. She did not look at East. She did not care what *he* thought.

"What I think," said Captain Safir after a long thoughtful pause, "is that someone wants us to believe that."

"Like who?" said Roxanna sourly, shooting hate glances at him. He could *never* agree with her.

"It wouldn't be a single person," said Per. "Because it's been going on so long. It has to be a group of people, one that remains cohesive even after the original members are dead—like a corporation. This corporation wants it believed that there is such a thing as a native Aeolian. This analysis"—he held up the biopsy card—"is rubbish. How many times did that biopsy change hands? There was the robot that found the body, the police officer who brought it in, our charming friend Chief Del Fuego, the funeral parlor attendants, us, East, the doctor who did the analysis—there is no guaranteeing that what is printed on this card is the analysis of a Mort biopsy. It is merely what someone wants us to believe is a Mort biopsy. And the doctor *did* say it looked manufactured."

"Why would anyone do that?" Roxanna argued.

"Land," said Per. "They aren't making it anymore. That is the key to this entire affair. Since you cannot *buy* land, and if you're not in line to inherit it, what better way to acquire it than to make rightful claim to it under interstellar law? Once this group establishes the existence of these so-called Aeolians, their next step will be to claim the planet in the name of the natives. And who would be better equipped to arrange the appearance of native Aeolians than the *designers* of Aeolis? Who else would have the expertise to tamper with the UBC's brain to obscure the identities of the Morts?—who *I* think are Earthlings. Who else would know how to get around the screens and scanners that they themselves designed? It has got to be someone involved with Aeolis since discovery, because the Morts started appearing as soon as this planet was discovered—and *not before*. There were no dead bodies waiting for the original discoverers, not even skeletons. The Morts *came with the Earthlings*. So who could arrange all that but the company that designed and developed Aeolis?

"What do you think, East?"

East rose and pulled out Laure's chair for her. "I am getting out of here before you get me arrested," he said. He was supposed to be keeping Laure out of trouble, not dragging her into it, and he had no love for the Service. "How did I let you get me into this, Roxanna?"

Roxanna sat back with her drink. "It's that ring through your nose with the sign that says *Pull*."

East reached for his hat, which was not there, darted an irritated glance at Laure, and escorted her toward the door.

"See you, East," said Roxanna.

"I hope not," said East and went out.

Per growled at Roxanna, "Now you've alienated our one ally."

"No I haven't. He loves it."

"What do *you* think of my idea?" he said, there being no one else to ask.

"Sir, it stinks."

They glowered at each other across the table, neither willing to consider the other's theory—or consider that perhaps the natives could not return.

For they had never left.

4/20/225 *Drina Village,*

New Europe, Northern, Aeolis

The mansion doors all along the promenade were left wide to the cooling breezes, and the gentry walked down the lanes arm in arm, some carrying lanterns. It was night this side of the world, and it was Indian summer.

A horse-drawn carriage clopped down one of the non-pedestrian avenues, the horses' tack aglow with lighted balls, looking like something out of a fairy kingdom.

Three days before their premiere, Niki Thea was escorting Mercedes back to Candle-in-the-Wind, the place Niki had arranged with one of his patrons for Mercedes to stay at—a chalet in a forest. He did not put his arm around her, though there was a wind, but walked by her side without touching.

They turned down a dark secluded lane. The only sounds were their heels on red brick, the rustling of leaves disturbed by an autumn zephyr, and the weird voices of night birds.

"They say there are witches and vampires on Aeolis," Mercedes said. The glowlamps were dim on this stretch of the path, and gnarled tree branches seemed about to reach out and seize passersby. The season was changing, and dead leaves flitted on the air like vampire bats.

"No. No witches and vampires," said Niki. Deep-brown eyes were solemn. His face was smooth and uncreased as if he never smiled, never frowned, never furled his brow, expressive yet still as an ivory carving. "Only spirits—and a few Outcast monsters, but those are very rare. Maybe they are all dead by now."

"Don't frighten me," said Mercedes. In daylight Niki sounded mad. At night with the wind howling Mercedes was less sure. "The way you say it makes a person almost believe it," she murmured.

"Do believe it, for they are here."

Mercedes shivered and pulled her shawl around her. "Will they hurt us?"

"Not me. Some of them might hurt you. You can talk to them, though most of them do not understand Earth languages."

"What do they speak?"

"A dead language."

Mercedes thought it a very poor joke, but then recognized that Niki had not intended it to be funny. Niki had no sense of humor.

He then told Mercedes a phrase to say if ever she felt menaced by the spirits. It was difficult for her to pronounce the sounds, but she mastered the odd words, wondered what kind of incantation from what kind of cult they were. She was aware that odd things went on in Aeolian cellars. "What am I saying?" she asked.

" 'Please don't hurt me,' " said Niki. "No spirit will harm you if you say that. They may even look after you."

"Why? Is it a charm?"

Niki looked irritated as if she spoke so much nonsense. "Because they would understand you for once."

A howling swelled in the trees, and a gust of wind swept down the lane. Mercedes shrank against Niki, who spoke a few strange words as if to command the winds away. The howling faded and the air calmed as if in obedience.

"The *wind*," Mercedes whispered. She shivered, eyes wide, looking around her at the stilled black forest. "Why do the dead haunt here?" she asked.

"Dead!" said Niki. "They are very much alive!"

4/20/225

Babylon, Little Asia, Northern, Aeolis

Found!

When Leader was yanked out of the garden where he had been fitfully sleeping, the only thought in his head was that the Earthlings had discovered his secret and that the Outcast, the Old Ones, and the Ancient Ones would all hold him responsible for it.

Then slowly he became aware that the Earthlings who had captured him had mistaken him for another Earthling, and he became thoroughly confused. They had found him naked and identityless like a Mort, but they failed to make the connection. And when they brought him before the Earthwoman called the duchess Estelita, she did not tell his captors to turn him over to the Service as Leader expected. Instead, she smiled slyly and said, "No ID? Then no one will miss him."

The remark made no sense, and since the Earthlings thought he was one of them, Leader could not understand what they wanted with him.

Why they had put him in this pit.

The pit was not very large, but its sides were very smooth and high, ringed with leering spectator-humans, and there was no way to climb out.

Desire to be gone tugged at Leader's fluttering heart, but even in mounting fear, he knew he had to remain in human form. These humans thought he was human. They must go on thinking so.

Suddenly a door slid open and a man entered the pit. Then the door slid shut again behind him, leaving no trace of a seam, no hope of escape.

The man held a knife.

Leader also held one—someone had placed it into his clammy hand before shoving him into the pit.

On seeing this armed man, Leader backed up flat against the wall, dropped his knife, and protested in a whispery voice that he did not want to do this. He was drowned out by hisses and exhortations of the spectators to make him fight for his life.

Leader froze, glassy-eyed, and the man lunged at him.

Instead of fainting or screaming, Leader acted with equal unthinking stupid fear and changed into his creature.

Instantly there was a small deerlike animal where Leader had been. It dodged out from under the knife attack, then sprang out of the pit with a strong thrust of its hind legs and landed in the midst of a crowd of humans. Its hoofs sliding on the smooth floor, it scrambled through a moving forest of legs amid shrieking grabbing uproar. Hands. Many snatching human hands.

More from impulse than conscious will, the creature changed form again, matter dissolving to essence so that it was nothing more than energy, no longer seen, but felt.

As wind.

Part Two:
KISTRAAL

Chapter I.
The Way of the World

Earth years 10,000 B.C. to 2318 A.D.
                              Kistraal (*Aeolis*)

While the ancestors of the Earthlings, who would revive a planet and rename it Aeolis, were still at the dawn of their civilization, humanoids of the planet Kistraal were near the sunset of theirs—or the eclipse, for their end was not in the normal cycle of things.

At a time when Aeolis was still called Kistraal, there lived beings who had evolved to be strikingly like Earthlings. But, as they had no concept of divinity, they had no basis for supposing that their natural form was inviolable, and they saw no reason not to make improvements.

Until they made a mistake.

In one nation, on the continent the Earthlings would call Northern, where humanoids were slender and dark-eyed, there was inadvertently created the first nonorganic life form in known existence.

The creation had been intended to be a humanoid that could change into an animal form at will, but, in changing, there was a stage in between in which the creation was something *else*. That stage, instead of being only a bridge between two physical organic forms, was a startling life form in itself, one of sentient energy, which could maintain itself indefinitely, retaining the identity and the memory of its physical forms. It thought and it had a will. It could not *see*, for it had no eyes, it could not *hear*, for it had no ears, but it *perceived* and could communicate with others in its state.

After a while it became evident that the creations were not simply single entities having three forms, but they were single entities having three *lives*, for each form was physically independent of the other two. Whatever the being experienced in one form had no physical bearing on the others. Wounds inflicted on one physical form did not affect the other; food to one did not stay the other's hunger. And while a being existed in one form, the others did not age. The only thing all three seemed to share was a common memory—and death. When one form died, they all died, though a being at the brink of death in one form could save himself by changing into one of the other two.

Because they had three lives, they outlasted their creators, and it was for later generations to discover just how long these mistakes would live. The humanoid form had a lifespan of forty to fifty years. Added to that was the lifespan of the animal form, ten to thirty years. Then there was the lifespan of the inorganic form, which their creators could not guess and did not live long enough to verify. Neither did the generation after them. Nor after *them*.

The inorganic form—the wind form—simply did not die until it *felt* like it. With both human form and animal form on the brink of death, the being could live as long as it pleased in its wind form—provided it did not yield to the temptation to return to one of its physical forms "one last time," linger an instant too long, and die with it. Unless they wanted to, or grew careless, the mistakes did not die.

And they did not seem to realize that they were mistakes. They multiplied.

Only the human forms were fertile, but if the tri-lived beings intended to survive as a people—and they did—they could not ignore their animal forms when thinking about children, for fertile children were born only to parents having the same animal form. A caste system arose in their closed society, divided by animal form, twenty castes to maintain twenty pure—fertile—strains. Mating outside one's caste became the worst crime one could commit, for the birth of too many mules could mean the death of their kind. The penalty would have been death if they could have figured out how to keep a convicted criminal in physical form long enough to execute him. Instead, the worst punishment they could devise was the casting out. Both the criminals and the crime, the unfortunate mule, were expelled from the closed society and treated as if they did not and never had existed. And if the outcasts had any sense at all they would commit suicide and make their nonexistence official.

Under such a system the beings flourished, having little in common with single-lived humanoids and having little to do with them—except that some of the beings were inordinately nosy and delighted in knowing secrets they would never tell. What one of them knew was that a second inorganic life form had been created in another nation, on another continent, a bigger mistake than the first one and worse for being intentional.

Something terrible, a mistake but not an accident. It was all it had been intended to be, a living weapon.

It was a non-carbon-based microorganism. Its creators knew it was alive because it moved, it consumed, and it reproduced itself at a terrifying rate—terrifying because what it consumed was carbon.

Then there was a war. No one knew exactly what happened because it happened so fast. Either the laboratory containing the microorganism was damaged or someone purposely freed the living weapon that could not be controlled or recaptured once freed.

And only the mistakes survived.

When the catastrophe struck, the only life that was safe was the nonorganic kind—the microorganism itself, and the wind forms. The living winds "saw" the rest of the world disintegrate into an eon of nothingness, and all that was left was soil, water, carbon-depleted air, and inorganic skeletons of cities.

The winds blew, covering the cities and the last traces of the old life.

As long as the wind forms had the will to live, nothing could harm them, but there was no rest, no sleep, no escape from thought but to die. If one wanted blissful oblivion it had to be forever. Many died out of boredom or despair, dissipating to nothing. Others reincarnated to their humanoid form and immediately fell victim to the microorganism, which also did not die with time but went into a dormant state and waited.

The Kistraalians who endured the best were those whose physical forms were already spent and so close to death that they could never reincarnate even if the catastrophe had not come to pass. They thought and exchanged thoughts—none of those thoughts having anything to do with ever walking on firm ground again. They sculpted the tortured shapes of the Ledges, and they sang through the Cave of the Winds, and they made the ashes of their world dance. This was how they assumed life would be. Forever.

Millennia passed, and Earth's civilizations rose and fell; the winds of Kistraal swept a barren world with no idea that their state would ever change. There was nothing to indicate that they were not alone in the universe.

Then in the terrestrial year 2153 A.D. the winds perceived the coming of the Earthships with a feeling of wonder so profound they almost conceived the concept of Deity.

Because neither of Kistraal's remaining life forms was carbon-based, they did not register on the Earthlings' scanners as living beings, so the planet was pronounced lifeless by the discoverers. And because the original explorers were secure inside inorganic ships, the microorganism did not detect them either, and so did not consume them.

But though the planet appeared safe to the Earthlings, there were just enough anomalies for them to blast it through with a sterilizing ray before venturing down.

The steray killed the microorganism. But it could not kill the winds.

When the winds perceived the Earthlings—humanoids much like they themselves had been—emerge from their ships, walk upon the ground, and breathe the air, they hardly dared believe. The Kistraalians swirled around the pioneer ships in their thousands, just to be near these humans.

The first voice to sound on Kistraal in ten thousand years, an American one, said, "Damned windy."

After that more ships came, hundreds of them, bringing people who at first explored with machines and puzzled at the abundance of free carbon—all that was left of the creation that destroyed the world after the steray struck it.

The Earthlings pumped carbon dioxide into the atmosphere, then brought green plants, mammals that ran across the plains, birds that soared and sang and waltzed with the winds, and fish that lived beneath their waters. And the Kistraalians at last knew the world was safe again.

It was not long after the coming of the Earthlings that the first Morts appeared—the untraceable, naked, aged corpses—the bodies of beings who wanted to die human in this paradise after a long long journey—and they were no longer consumed by the microorganism when they chose to do so.

The Kistraalians who were still able dared to resume their physical forms after ten thousand years. There were only a scant two thousand of them, the vast majority too old to produce children. And all of them, once they had breathed again, slept again, touched the ground, and loved again, could not go back to their wind form—ever. It was almost a physical impossibility. They would rather die. So they did, leaving behind five hundred children. The next generation was little more than two hundred, the next fifty. And so it dwindled to the last, like a small colony of pioneers, unprotected on a new world, who didn't quite make it. Miscarriage, infant death, too many males, trangressions of caste lines, sickness, and need of hospitals that were ten thousand years ash—the Kistraalians could see what was killing them but could not do much to stop it. Kistraal had died long ago. This place was Aeolis.

Everything had changed. They themselves had a new hierarchy in their society, because their society was so different from what it had been. The most revered of their kind were now the ones called the Ancient Ones—those who had made the ten-thousand-year Crossing.

Next were the Old Ones, those born after the Crossing who had lived out their physical lives and had joined the Ancient Ones as wind.

Next would be the Young Ones, those born after the Crossing who still had physical life in them. But there were no more of these left to be called Young Ones.

Last were those who should have been Young Ones but whose only association with society was that they were defined by their exclusion from it: the Outcast.

The worst punishment among the Kistraalians was still, more than ever, the casting out. There were twenty-four who had, according to the code of the Kistraalians, done something to deserve it.

There were two kinds of crimes: crimes of doing and crimes of being. Crimes of doing could be murder—such as Aquilla, Mer, Phytho, and the Pleiades had committed—or crossing caste lines, which was murdering the People—such as Scorpii, Pega, and Mona had done.

The other ten Outcast were guilty of crimes of being. They were the mules and freaks. The actual crime they suffered for was that of their parents, but it made no difference.

The Outcast maintained a feeble hierarchy of their own, also based on age, for Kistraalians equated old age with strength.

Oldest of the Outcast was Leader, but he was old out of fear, not strength. All his life he had spent little time in his humanoid form, which could not endure the light and was terrified of darkness. So, although he was nearly a hundred years old, his human form had barely aged out of boyhood.

Now Leader forced himself to stay in human form. Ever since he had become Leader he spent as much time as possible in physical form, trying to grow old as fast as possible—because he did not want to be the last one left, and he hadn't the courage to kill himself.

He hugged his knees and cowered in the Cave of the Winds. Every time he closed his eyes he saw a knife coming toward him, and every time he opened his eyes he remembered what he had done. He had shown the Earthlings exactly what sort of beings were here on Aeolis with them. He had changed forms before Earthlings—before the one called the duchess, which seemed to be the Earthling term for "Leader."

Leader sent Leo to see what the Service was making of it, but Leo reported that the Service was apparently oblivious, for the captain was tossing darts and the other two officers were playing a board game, the woman moaning about her dead bagpipes, whatever sort of creature that was.

Don't these Earthlings talk to each other? Leader wondered, baffled. The Earthlings were like a creature at cross-purposes with itself: one eye watched and searched, while the other eye was sealed shut; one hand dug and probed while the other hand hid and buried.

I don't understand Earthlings. Not at all.

He remembered what the old Leader had said to him: *The Earthlings are trying very hard not to know.* Half of them were, anyway. And luckily for Leader, the people who had seen him change were among that half. But Leader could not know that.

He buried his head in his arms, exhausted from terror, and fell asleep.

And dreamed.

A wall of darkness like night overtaking the world once and for all.

Tried to change form but could not.

Tried to run. Like running in water.

The void overtaking him. Something inside told him this was the thing that destroyed the world.

Came to a cliff. Jumped and tried to fly, tried to become wind.

But just kept falling.

Awareness that this was a dream, but remembering that he had once been told that if he saw himself die in a dream he would really die.

Fall to rocks. Body breaking upon the stone.

Dying.

And woke screaming.

He felt hands upon him, rock beneath him, saw only blackness, and it was some moments before he realized that he was awake and there was someone with him smoothing back his dirty hair, caressing his thrashing limbs, and telling him he was safe.

It was a woman. He knew her by her musky smell. Scorpii. "Just a dream," she murmured in a low sweet voice. "Just a dream. I am here. You are safe."

Leader relaxed with a whimpered sigh and melted into her soft embrace. Her skin was warm, almost hot to touch, and her thick hair draped over both of them, forming a safe private cocoon.

"Scorpii—" he whispered hoarsely. "The Earthlings—"

But her small finger passed over his lips and she said, "You don't know Earthmen as I do. They will believe what they will to believe. If you changed form in the middle of the spaceport instead of a gladiators' den, it would be no different."

"The Service—"

"The Earthlings themselves will take care of the Service," she said. A soothing hand closed his eyes. "Sleep, Leader. Your dreams will be sweet this time, I promise you."

He could not have stayed wakeful had he tried, and he was asleep again almost instantly, dreaming the strangest dreams of being with a woman and of things he had never done.

Vividly.

Chapter II.
Dance

4/23/225

Des Vaux Estate, New Europe, Northern, Aeolis

Roxanna Douglas returned to the Des Vaux estate because she did not know where else to begin to look. What to look for, she did not know either. She had been on the planet nearly two Aeolian months, during which time she had succeeded in finding a dragon, a lost civilization, and a body that seemed manufactured—none of which was what anyone wanted to hear.

Two months. The Aeolian month was an arbitrary twenty-nine days, having nothing whatever to do with the planet's three moons, and, in Earth time, an Aeolian day lasted twenty-five hours and twelve minutes, just different enough to be irritating.

Roxanna wandered over the grounds, brooding. The long day was ending, but, though the sun was nearly out of sight, Indian summer had come to this latitude and it was warmer than when she had been here last. She folded her Service jacket over her arm and walked into the surrounding woods called Forêt Noir.

The forest was thick with all the golden autumn flowers and with deep-fissured black oaks holding fast to their dead brown leaves.

She walked on for some time until it was fully night. She had come to descending ground, and the trees had changed to ghostly white birches and the drooping shapes of willows.

Then the forest broke, and she was standing at the bank of a woodland lake, the surface perfectly still, a mirror to the clear sky almost bright with starlight. Across the water where willows trailed their limbs in the shallows she saw an antlered head rise suddenly, then retreat into the gloom. She did not move, and the crickets and frogs that had silenced at her approach began to sing again.

Roxanna gazed across the waters, felt like sighing, then glanced about. She was completely alone. She looked at the water, looked back down the path she had come, then back to the water.

She took off her clothes and waded in. When she was in up to her chin she passed a spread hand through the water, felt it swirl between her fingers, and small eddies fan off and whisper against her thigh. A closed hand was enough to move her off her feet, and like a bird flying for the first time she didn't look back.

She swam naturally, never taught, the element itself commanding a certain way of moving, and a lazy sidestroke was what she came up with. It never occurred to her to thrash.

Out toward the center, the lake was cool and deep, and Roxanna stopped, figuring out that she could keep her face above the surface simply by lying back.

Then she became motionless, gazing up at millions of stars, seeing more of them the longer she looked, the sky glowing with them, but if she focused directly on a single one she could not see it at all, the human retina not being well organized for stargazing.

She waited for a falling star, but then realized that none would be coming—meteoroids could not pass through Aeolis's defense screen.

So, Aeolis, you can't have everything, Roxanna thought.

She took a few lazy strokes.

But you're awfully close.

Floating on her back with her ears underwater she did not hear footsteps approach. When she raised her head and began to sidestroke again, she was taken by surprise by a voice from the lake's edge, chanting:

"Scorpion, sting not.

I would do your bidding.

But flesh is flesh, a man am I,

Give me time this time.

Allay, anek, aga a."

"What the hell are you talking about?" Roxanna said to the figure on the bank.

There was a pause. "You're not the Scorpion witch."

"No."

"Who are you then?"

"I'm a flesh-and-blood trespasser."

"Oh."

Roxanna swam back toward the bank till she could distinguish the form of a young lad in lackey's garb. He was standing near her clothes.

Roxanna had little trust for young males, and, as she had no desire to risk returning to the *Halcyon* naked, she decided to retrieve her uniform right then. She rose out of the water, and the lad modestly closed his eyes.

"What made you think I was this Scorpion witch?" Roxanna asked, getting dressed.

"She's always, um, naked, she's light-skinned, her hair is black—"

Roxanna smirked. "My hair is auburn," she said.

The lackey replied without opening his eyes, "Lady, I don't know what color it is dry, but it's black now."

Roxanna held a strand before her eyes. Water baths were for the wealthy, and she was not used to being wet or noticing what water did to her hair color. "You have a point there," she conceded. She put her Service hat on. "You can open your eyes."

He did and immediately snapped to attention and saluted, "Ma'am!"

"At ease, for God's sake," she said. "You used to be in the Service."

"Yes, ma'am. That's how I got this job," he said proudly. "I was an escort for Count Mirov's entourage. He liked my attitude."

Subservience becomes you, thought Roxanna. "Who is this Scorpion witch?"

The lackey shrugged. "She's a succubus—only she doesn't come to you in dreams. If you don't give her her way, she sets her scorpion on you."

"What is 'her way'?"

"Well, ma'am, um . . ."

"I see," said Roxanna. "You've seen the scorpion?" There were no scorpions on Aeolis.

"Yes, ma'am. It's big as a cat." The lad was obviously

raised off-world. There were no cats on Aeolis either. "It's purple and hairy—fringy-like hair—"

"That is like no scorpion *I* ever heard of," said Roxanna.

"And it has four legs," the lad added.

Roxanna shook her head. "Why do you call it a scorpion, then?"

"It's shaped like one, and its tail—look out for its tail. It comes out of thin air. So does she."

"Thin air?"

"Stranger things have happened here," the boy said defensively.

"Tell it to my jeep," Roxanna muttered.

"Ma'am?"

I've found something else. What have I found? She did believe him. *Buddy's succubus. But what is she?*

"Nothing," she said distractedly.

She could not help feeling that the woman, the succubus, was related to the dragon somehow, and that she was after something. Besides the obvious.

4/23/225

Ledges, New Africa, Southern, Aeolis

Leader was usually to be found outside when twilight came, sitting on a sandstone ledge still warm from the day. So when Leo stepped out of the air, materializing from his wind form to skip over the rocks in search of Leader, he knew which places to look. But had he known Leader might not be alone, Leo would never have materialized, would never have let his presence be known, and would have left immediately. But Leader was always alone, so Leo was not expecting it when he climbed up a low rise, looked over the summit, and two pairs of eyes looked back.

Leo stopped.

Leader was cross-legged on the ground, Scorpii kneeling behind him, closer than she need be, cutting his hair. Actually she was done cutting it and was just playing with it. Her touch stayed gentle, but her eyes became suddenly hard and glared malevolently over Leader's head, boring into Leo's.

Leader was looking at him expectantly, too innocent to know he was being devoured. "Yes, Leo?" he whispered.

Scorpii kept her hands on Leader in ownership, her dark hair curtaining both of them, her eyes commanding Leo not to speak.

Leo's whiskers twitched. He did his best to ignore Scorpii and spoke to Leader. "Do you remember seven years ago there was an Earthling dancer I wanted to see? You said you would go with me?"

"Yes," said Leader. "But he quit."

"He has come back. He opens today. Will you come with me?"

"Today?"

"Before he gets away again. The dance starts soon. The theater is two hours to the east." Leo referred to geographical time zones as hours, though as wind he could be there in a matter of minutes. "I don't want to miss him again. Someday he will disappear and never come back."

Leo adored civilization, and the arts were the zenith of civilization to him. Himself he considered the nadir.

Leader whispered, "Of course I will go with you."

Scorpii waited, impatience showing in her hands, and at last she spoke with strained casualness. "Aren't you going to ask me, Leader?"

"Ask you what?" Leader looked at her over his shoulder.

She caressed his chinline. "If I want to go with you."

"Do you?" Leader asked, ignorant of the byplay that went on over his head.

"No," she said, and got up and changed to wind.

Leader turned to Leo. "Is she angry?"

Leo shook his head, as some Earthlings did when exasperated. Leader interpreted the gesture as a negative. Leader could be very stupid when he chose to be. He was not quite aware of what was happening to him. He had been a boy for the past one hundred years, and innocence was so ingrained it was almost permanently fixed.

"Be careful of her," said Leo. "She will hurt you."

Leader was bewildered. "Why? How? We are all wind."

Leo shook his head again. *She can sting to death anyone she pleases.*

4/23/225 Gem Theater,

Drina Village, New Europe, Northern, Aeolis

As close to love as Niki ever got, with more passion and burning intensity than most ever gave in an act of love, Niki danced, concentrating all energy into each movement, each flowing into each with the smoothness of a wave, yet each clean and contained as a beam of light. And when Mercedes was in his focus she felt she would burn to ash as a mortal woman who dared look upon a god in his epiphany. But Mercedes refused to wither away as if Niki were the only one on stage. When he looked at her with all that fire, she met his gaze full in the eyes, showing everything she felt with her own strong vulnerability, as if she might touch his pride. The dance became an exchange of strengths, each reflecting each brighter than before.

Yes, I am lovely. She saw it in his face, felt it within herself. She felt light, carried by the music, the great effort effortless, and she was touched by a mystic and not quite rational feeling that she had tapped into—*eye hath not seen, nor ear heard*—something, a power, a joy beyond conception, not to be expressed by laughter or tears or anything but dance.

Impossibly beautiful and transitory as all beautiful things, the dance ended, and Mercedes felt more drained, weak, and dizzy than ever in love.

The audience was on its feet, and for the rest of the troupe, this was the moment of glory. For Mercedes hers was over, and Niki was oblivious to the thunder. He faced the audience, but his gaze was up and beyond the spotlights, toward the rafters, as if heeding another kind of applause.

Mercedes looked up also—to where the air above the audience unmistakably—

—glittered.

Leo and Leader were not in the theater. They had come, only to find the house filled with Ancient Ones and Old Ones crowding the rafters so thickly that the air crackled and sparked, all of them drawn to the universal appeal of the dance.

The two Outcast, not feeling at ease among their elders and their betters, fled.

They would see Niki Thea another time.

4/23-4/225

Gem Theater, Drina Village, New Europe,
Northern, Aeolis

Mercedes left the theater with Niki very late and feeling the effects of too much champagne. Despite all they had done together, the shared passion, Niki seemed as oblivious as ever to Mercedes the woman, or even to Mercedes anything but the dancer.

She searched for his thoughts on his face, but his expression was ambiguous as always—lips slightly parted, fine arched brows high, making him look wide-eyed, wistful, sometimes quizzical—or, when his eyes were closed, rapt.

He came to a stop just outside the theater.

A hologram had appeared in the outer courtyard, recorded during the opening performance, capturing an instant when Mercedes was up on toe in an arabesque before Niki, their gazes intimate, her hands almost touching his chest. It was a dynamic moment, even the frozen image unable to rob the figures of their life. They were beautiful together.

Niki walked around the hologram, regarding it critically, and Mercedes feared he was going to correct her position, but at last he nodded and said, "You are great because you love the dance and it shows."

That was the breaking point. How could he come so close yet miss entirely? Mercedes threw her hands down to her sides and blurted out, "I love *you*, you . . . dumbhead!"

Niki looked puzzled.

Mercedes sat down on a stone bench in the courtyard and burst into tears. This time she did not care if he saw it. She leaned over her knees, face in her hands and sobbed. "I didn't stay on Aeolis to dance. I can dance anywhere. I stayed because of *you*."

Niki stood by helplessly, distressed by the incomprehensible girl on the bench crying. He looked up at the sky as if expecting an answer would be written there. There were only the pale moons blinking in and out behind the clouds, and a flock of geese passing unseen, their rusty cries carried to him on a night wind. "I don't understand," said Niki.

"Ask your damned ghosts!" said Mercedes.

Niki cocked his head and listened. "They say—"

"*Oh!*" Mercedes cried and jumped to her feet. She had not meant for him to take her literally.

"What?" Niki asked, utterly confused and sincerely trying very hard to understand her.

His honest bewilderment was more than Mercedes could bear. She took a few backward steps. "Don't talk to me. Just *go away*. I can't take it anymore." And she fled.

"What did I do?" Niki cried to the ancient winds.

You want us to tell you about being human?

"What is wrong with her?"

She is in love with you.

"But she makes no sense."

She is more understandable than you are.

"I don't understand."

The winds voiced what amounted to a sigh. *Then none of us is going to be able to explain it to you. Just dance. That is your life.*

That should have satisfied him, for it was the answer to every question, but it did not. Not this time. He looked down the walk, took an ineffectual step the way she had gone. "She—" he began, but did not know what he was going to say about her.

"She . . ."

Chapter III.
Children

4/24/225

Ledges, New Africa, Southern, Aeolis

Leader had fallen asleep to odd dreams again. He woke to turbulence within, an intense feeling he was unused to. A woman's hand on him brought an involuntary reaction, and he tried to crawl away, embarrassed and barely awake.

"That is for me. You want me," Scorpii said, reaching to touch him, but Leader jerked back as if from her scorpion. He wanted to hide, but she had caught his wrist and held it. He choked out, "I—I'm sorry, Scorpii."

Her smile was both gentle and mocking. "Have you never?" The hand that held his wrist was small and soft, the grip firm and insistent.

"Scorpii, I—I—"

"You," she said in tender tease.

"I am not of your caste."

"I want your child, Leader."

"I'm a mule," he said. He felt his ears burn scarlet. Vague longings had never taken focus before in his complete ignorance, for sex was something he never let himself think about. He was not even exactly sure how it was *done*. Women were a mystery to him and not for mules to be concerned with.

"You are Leader."

"I am still a mule. I have not changed. I am still Pala."

"Leader," she insisted, voice very low. Her arms were around his neck.

Leader stumbled over words. "Scorpii, I would do anything in my power to give you a child. I just *can't*."

"So-called mules have had children before."

"It happened once," said Leader. "Once."

"So twice," she said. "Don't be afraid. I will show you how it is done."

"But I can't *do* anything," he cried.

"Yes, you can."

In absolute panic now, he broke away from her, needing to get away from her soft voice, soft hands, sweet smell, and what it was doing to him. He wanted her, but it was too deeply instilled that sex was for one thing only, and the idea of a mule's trying to make children was too obscene and ridiculous to be accepted.

"Leader . . ." Scorpii's tone changed, still urgent but appealing to reason more than desire. "We are the last ones who can save Kistraal. You have to help me. You must. You cannot turn our world over to the aliens just like that."

"There is nothing I can do about that," said Leader.

"There is. To own a world you must have someone to inherit it."

"The Earthlings are bearing no children here either," said Leader.

The Earthlings had been told that it was unwise to bear children on a sterile world. It would breed the immunity out of them so that later generations could never leave Aeolis. Aristocratic tradition then dictated that a child should be born in the country of its ancestors. And among Aeolians it had become improper to be seen pregnant. Some women hired other women to carry their babies to term off-planet. Dogs, after all, bore their own puppies. That was not for gentlefolk.

Aeolis was a sterile world indeed.

"But the Earthlings *have* had one child here," said Scorpii. "And everyone treats her like a native. Leader, I have to have a baby. I have to. Before they take the world from us. Come to me. Please help me."

He did not move, and she went to him. He let her touch him in places he had never been touched, and teach him what he did not know.

4/24/225 Remington Estate,

New Africa, Southern, Aeolis

East saw Laure safely back to her estate. To Stephen. East had accompanied her on a journey she feared, but that was behind her now and Stephen was the one she came home to. She greeted her husband as if she had been gone a long long time.

Not needed anymore, East was left to become sour-tempered.

Then one evening Laure peered into East's sanctuary. "I bought you a present," she said.

East grunted.

She walked around behind him where he sat at the table. "It's a peace offering, actually," she said, placing it on his head.

He took it off. It was a hat. It was not too horrible, very much like his old one in style, but it was *new*, not the comfortable old companion he had become used to and that was used to East. It was expensive and made from fine material, the kind East would never put out the money to buy himself.

"I have another surprise," said Laure.

"Is it better than this one?" said East, tossing the hat on the table.

"Don't be mean or I shan't tell you. It's a secret, really."

"What now?"

"No, I've changed my mind," she said and danced toward the door.

"Laure!" he thundered. She turned, startled by the authority in his voice, and that he should dare use that tone with her.

She quickly retaliated. "Yes, Daddy?" She knew which strings connected to his heart, and every once in a while gave a good strong yank to make sure he did not forget it.

East glared, truly angry. "Is this something I should know?" he demanded in even tones.

Laure's eyes flickered and she hesitated as if making a decision. "You are my bodyguard," she said.

"What, then?"

She shrugged one shoulder and turned on the ball of her foot to dance out. "I'm pregnant."

She looked back once to see if she had drawn blood. She had. Satisfied, she left him alone.

East felt his stomach kick, bitterness rise in his throat. He swallowed it back down hard. It left his throat stinging, mouth sour.

He moved stiffly to the bathroom, closed the door, and fell back against it. He thought he would be sick.

You stupid OLD man.

He leaned forward, bracing himself against the wall, hands on either side of a mirror, hanging his head, dizzy, breathing hard and fast. Then he lifted his head and saw his ugly face reflected back at him—the weathered hide, the homely features, all the wrinkles, all the scars, all the years. And he put his fist through the glass. It shattered in a spray pattern.

He staggered back, knuckles bleeding.

Almighty God, what do you want of me? Enough! God, God, God, God!

He threw back his head, eyes rolled upward, reeling under an assault on the spirit the body could not bear.

God!

He did not know how he had let himself come to this. He should have seen it coming—Laure and Stephen were, after all, married—but he somehow had not expected it. And he hadn't expected it to hit him this hard.

He leaned against a wall and slid down it till he was sitting on the floor, elbows on his knees, forehead resting on his palm heels.

Like saying, "Yes, East, I love my husband," she annihilated him with a word.

The thought of those two together was unimaginable; Stephen touching Laure was sacrilege. Beyond that was the unendurable thought of Laure carrying Stephen's child.

It should have been ours—another thought that sprang into his head unbidden and unwelcome.

He recalled his father's gentle persuasion—"When the hell are you ever going to make me some grandchildren—ones named East, that is!" Father was a hundred years old. He was getting impatient.

East smiled wryly, feeling closer to tears, but East never cried.

He lifted his head, took a deep breath, and sighed

voicelessly. He looked at his blooded knuckles and the shattered mirror. *Goddam real glass.*

He guessed he ought to clean his hand. The mirror he left for the servants.

For three days Laure mused out loud what she would name the child. If it was a boy, she confided to a friend, he would be a junior.

"Junior!" the friend cried. "Why should he only carry your husband's name? Laure, dear, it's a baby, not a *clone*."

But East, who was well within earshot, suspected that that piece of information had been spoken solely for his benefit.

And on the fourth day he began to suspect that a lot more than just the name had been staged simply for him, when Laure told her friend, "False alarm."

She had not seen a doctor, and her husband seemed ignorant of the matter, so East guessed the whole charade had been aimed at him. He wondered if she had ever thought she was pregnant at all. If she had meant to hurt him, she had succeeded very well.

He was alternately relieved and angered, but too drained and shaken to either rejoice or retaliate—as if it were actually within his power to retaliate, for he could not hurt her if she did not care, and she obviously did not.

The mirror in the bathroom had been replaced, and the man he saw in it looked haggard.

It was then that he ran into the maidservant in his sanctuary checking the serving machines. East had been running into her a lot of late, but he had never noticed her before or stopped to consider that she crossed his path more often than could be accidental—a buxom, sweet-scented, black-haired woman with blue eyes and cupid-bow mouth. Her name was Rivke, and she made much of East's injured knuckles. She took his hand in both of hers, drew it to her lips, kissed it, then flicked her warm tongue over his fingers.

She was too well-used to really suit East, but he was in the mood for a woman to be kind, and Rivke soothed his battered pride and caressed his raw nerves. "Where I come from you are a damned good-looking man. We like our men *men*. I never saw a man so strong." She let her small fingers intertwine with his big callused ones.

East lifted her hand, kissed her fingertips, and held her

palm to his rough cheek. Her breasts rose with a deep inhalation and strained against the confines of her bodice. "I thought you would never look at me," she breathed. "I'm at least as pretty as La Laure."

East almost told her not to push her luck, stung both by the slight to Laure and the fact that his idiotic infatuation was that obvious. But he did not say anything to her at all, just let her lead him to her bed, and did something he had never done with a woman—closed his eyes and pretended she was someone else.

In the morning East was confronted by Laure, who was furious with him. Her reaction left East a little confused. He had done nothing out of line, for servants did it all the time with no one ever raising an eyebrow. East was bound to no one—and certainly not to Laure as anything but a bodyguard—so why was she objecting?

"Rats jump all over each other. Eagles fly in pairs," she said.

East would have been properly shamed—at least for the moment—had it not been for the ludicrous analogy of Stephen as an eagle. Himself as a rat and Laure as a soaring monarch of the air he could buy, but *not* Stephen. So he laughed.

And Laure's eyes flashed as her dart failed.

"I'll have my husband fire you," she said.

East stopped laughing, startled, not that she was threatening to fire him, but that he had inadvertently turned the tables on her. She was *jealous*. He had exacted his revenge, and he had not even meant to. It was his game now, for once. "And what will you say when he asks why?" he asked.

Laure flushed crimson in fury. She had betrayed herself, and badly. East had hated last night, but that reaction made it all worth it.

The lady tried awkwardly to recover her position. "I expect you to behave better than my other servants," she improvised, excusing her anger as *anything* but jealousy, as if she could not possibly care. "I am, after all, seen with you."

"As you say." East smiled and inclined his head slightly, very polite, but his blue eyes glinted as hers did whenever she scored a victory.

"It is just that I forget to think of you as an inferior class sometimes," she added, trying to reestablish her dominance—like trying to resurrect the dead. "But I guess low-class will always be low-class. It is sometimes startling—and disappointing—to be reminded."

"Of course," said East.

"And stop condescending to me or I *will* have you fired."

"Yes, ma'am," said East.

No amount of her objecting could change the fact that this round belonged to him.

4/27/225 Remington Estate,
New Africa, Southern, Aeolis

East halted outside the parlor on hearing Stephen speaking within. "Laure, darling, you fired a servant?"

Laure's reply was harsh. "I don't have to consult with you on every little household transaction, do I? I don't have to account to you for everything I do."

East immediately knew who had been fired, but could not see why. This was an erratic move. It could not be aimed at him this time, for he could not care less whether the girl stayed or went. Yet it had to connect to him somehow.

How?

He could hear Stephen backing down, making apologies. "Of course you don't, dear. I was just surprised, that's all. I couldn't imagine why—"

"She's a nasty little girl and I don't like her."

East waited until Stephen left and Laure was alone to come out into the parlor.

Laure saw him and turned her back to walk away, but he caught up with her with two big strides and closed his hand very firmly on her upper arm, stopped her and made her face him. Her dark eyes were fierce, her wide mouth curled in angry defiance.

"Why did you fire Rivke?" East said, low and firm.

But he guessed why even as he asked—and belief followed slowly. Her jealously ran much deeper than he had thought. And there was much more underneath it than he dared hope.

Seeing that he knew, her eyes damned him and her thin lip trembled. "Because I couldn't kill her!" Laure cried, and broke away and ran.

Chapter IV.
Dattas Rising

5/2/225

The Ledges, New Africa, Southern, Aeolis

The first thing Draco did on finding Leader and Scorpii together was laugh.

Leader and Scorpii?

The second was to have sex with Scorpii in front of Leader—or at least start in front of Leader, for Leader left very quickly on seeing what was happening.

When Draco was finished with Scorpii, he sought out Leader and cornered him. "Do you want to try to cast me out again, Leader?" said Draco, smelling strongly of Scorpii's sweet musky scent.

"No," said Leader.

Draco put an arm around Leader's shoulders. "Shall I tell you something?"

"No."

Draco told him anyway. "You picked the wrong female to give your heart to. Scorpii would do it with a tree if she thought it would get her pregnant."

Leader said nothing.

"Leader, I liked you better before," said Draco. "You used to be so malleable. Lately you have been acting as if you thought you were really a leader. You were due for a squashing. You see that, don't you?"

"No."

"My dragon is going to live," said Draco.

"That is good news," said Leader.

"Is it? You hoped it would die."

"No, I didn't."

"Leo said you did."

"When did you ever believe Leo?" Leader said.

"Admit it, my dragon frightens you."

"That does not mean I want it dead."

"It is recovering," said Draco. "And it is hungry."

"Draco—" Leader started, alarmed, the first real reaction Draco had been able to draw out of him.

"There are millions of Earthlings," said Draco. "Someone has to keep them from spreading."

"Draco."

"They are so funny when their eyes bug and their little mouths drop open—"

"Draco, they are *just like us!*" Leader rasped. If only he could make Draco see it as murder. Draco did not consider himself a murderer, though it did not bother him to be viewed as one. He seemed to relish it.

Draco responded slowly, "I did make a mistake when the dragon ate that Earthman."

"I am glad you see that," said Leader.

"Yes, there was a witness. But it turned out all right—she killed herself."

"*Draco!*"

Draco smiled and kissed Leader on the forehead. "Goodbye, Leader."

It was a ritual kiss for the dying.

"Me. You're going to eat me," Leader said dully.

"Not yet. Later. I must go now."

"Draco, please."

"You have nothing to worry about."

"I don't?"

Draco grinned and explained, "No witnesses this time."

5/2/225 *Candle-in-the-Wind,*

Drina Village, New Europe, Northern, Aeolis

Mercedes nestled in an overstuffed chair with a very large pillow and an oversized afghan, listening to a recording of French lute music and trying to read a book. She was alone. She had told Niki to stay away, and so he had. He had not said a word to her since her outburst. The only time she had any contact with him now was during performances. She was too professional to carry private conflicts into a dance, and in that oasis of light on the stage she came alive again, each time new, each time the first, the best. But the comedown from such great heights after each performance was an abysmal drop, and the impact at the bottom created a depression of great depth for her to wallow in. So she would come back to Candle-in-the-Wind by herself and comfort herself with music.

The lute recording ended. The silence after sound was deep, oppressive, encircling, penetrating, isolating. She had all the lights turned on but could not dispel the feeling of gray.

Alone and lonely, she wanted to call someone, but she had cut herself off from the only person in the world that she knew.

The only thing to do was to go to bed quickly.

She turned out all the lights and dove under the covers. She had kept the chalet cold, for she liked to sleep under many blankets, drink hot drinks, hold purring cats, and warm her hands in someone else's. But the latter two things she had been unable to do since coming to Aeolis.

When she finally managed to fall into a fitful sleep, a phone chimed. She jumped out of bed, thinking it might be Niki, though it was unlike him to forget the difference in time zones. She searched for the phone, groggy and unable to tell where the chimes were coming from. Once upon a time when phones had cords one could at least find them.

She did find it, snatched it up, but the expected hologram of Niki did not form in the room. No image formed at all. The sender did not have his video on.

"Hello?" said Mercedes.

A non-Japanese voice began to speak Japanese badly, like someone without a language nodule, and it took Mercedes a moment to realize that it was a threatening call.

She slammed down the phone and burrowed back into the bed, the covers pulled over her head.

A phone chimed. Different chime. Different phone.

She was awake by now and afraid.

Niki, that had better be you.

She answered the other phone.

No video. Same voice. She hung up. She stood and stared at the phones. Eventually one rang again. She picked up both, intending to call the police on the one not occupied, but she couldn't, and it was all she could do to keep from screaming.

The voice came over both phones. The caller was somewhere in the chalet, calling one phone from the other's extension.

She put down both phones, locked her bedroom door, picked up one phone—it was free now—and called the police. She could barely speak. "Hur-ry, some-one is in here right now!"

They arrived within a minute, activated the front door lock with a police key, and let themselves in.

"Miss, are you all right?" an officer called from the first floor.

"Yes, I'm up here," she cried through the closed bedroom door.

"Turn around, pretty lady," a voice from behind her hissed in bad Japanese. She whirled to face an intercom. She shut it off and called through the door to the police, "He's still in the house!"

She heard the sound of many officers moving about and one climbing the steps. "Miss?" It was a female voice.

Mercedes opened the door to a very tall policewoman. "Did you find him?" asked Mercedes, unable to stop shaking.

"Not yet, but don't worry," said the officer. She held something small that looked like a weapon in her hand. She looked at Mercedes and her expression changed. "You're Mercedes Stokolska, the dancer."

"Yes, ma'am." Mercedes was able to smile, still trembling.

"I'm sorry this had to happen to you," said the officer. "There really aren't too many warped types on this planet. I don't know why he picked you. Are you alone here?"

"Yes, ma'am."

"*That's* why." She nodded. "Yours is probably the only house in the world without a servant."

I could name one other.

A lieutenant joined the policewoman. "He's gone."

"Are you sure?" said Mercedes.

The lieutenant turned on a scanner and showed it to her. "See, eight people are registering. Seven of us and one of you. He's not in the house. We're securing all the doors and windows for you so he can't get back in."

Mercedes nodded. "Thank you."

But she stayed up long after the police left, walking the halls, checking room to room, with all the lights on.

At last convinced that she was safe, she went back to bed.

Then she heard footsteps on the stairs.

Don't think. Don't freeze. Just move!

She flew out of the bed, seized up a phone, darted out of her bedroom to the head of the stairs, poised to hurl the phone at the intruder.

There was no one there.

She checked all the doors and windows once again. They were secure and undisturbed.

Weary and feeling sick, she returned to her room and collapsed.

And heard scratching at the window. She opened one eye and could have sworn she saw a hand reach through the curtains. She was still holding the phone, and she threw it. It bounced off the stormglass window.

She turned on the lights. Alone. Of course.

She debated calling the police again. *And tell them what? Ghosts?*

Too tired and frightened to feel silly, she spoke the words Niki had taught her: *"Don't hurt me."*

Nine heartbeats of silence, then abrupt booming laughter came from downstairs.

That was real!

She scrambled for the phone she had thrown.

And the shower in the adjacent bathroom suddenly turned on, and all Mercedes's muscles contracted on impulse.

Don't freeze. Don't freeze. She jumped through the door, phone raised. But she was alone with the running water.

She leaned against the wall. *I am going mad. Like Niki.*

She slid back the door to the shower stall and stifled a shriek.

Scrawled on the wall, almost illegible, it said: *Die, pretty lady.*

The lights went out behind her in the bedroom. She heard breathing. She slammed the bathroom door shut and locked it. She tried to use the phone, but she had broken it. The other one was still in the bedroom. She shut off the water, held her breath, and listened.

There was a scratch at the door and a slithering. She

looked down to see a long red whiplike *tongue* slide under the door.

She threw the phone on it.

A roar that shook the building exploded as the serpent tongue whipped back under the door.

Then there was silence again but for Mercedes's shallow gasping breath and thundering heartbeat.

Niki had not taught her what to say to Outcast monsters.

And a crash came from above as a serpent tail forced the stormglass skylight out of its casing, raining down splinters and crumbled molding, and it came writhing in.

Mercedes tore open the door to the bedroom, seized the other phone as she passed through, and ran down the stairs. She did not call the police. She called Niki.

Answer. God, make him answer.

She wanted to go down to the cellar to the tube car bay, but the closed door and what might lurk in the cellar frightened her. So she hid in the dining room under a table with a floor-length cloth, holding the phone to her.

Answer, God in heaven, answer.

A quiet irritated voice sounded from the phone. "Who is this? Where is your video?"

"Niki, help," Mercedes whispered into the phone.

"Mercedes?"

"Niki, help."

A movement of the tablecloth caught the corner of her eye. She shut off the phone and held her breath. *God, don't let it find me here.* She heard footsteps and breathing. Then nothing.

Suddenly she was out in the open as the entire table lifted up. She saw the serpent—splintering maplewood in its jaws, eyes glowing green in the dark, barring her last hope of escape, the cellar door.

Before she had time to think twice and freeze with panic, Mercedes took a flying leap through one of the beast's raised coils to the door and ran down the stairs to the tube car bay. If any place was safe, that was. The cars were airtight, and if she could just get inside, she could get out of the chalet faster than the speed of sound. The tube system would take her underground anywhere in the continent.

She flung open the bay door and almost plunged down a long drop into the tube tunnel.

The tube car was gone.

And that was all Mercedes could take. It was simply the end of all hope—for she became aware that the tunnel was not quite empty. She heard the breathing of something immense and reptilian inside, and saw a faint green bioluminescent glow rising into the bay.

She started to laugh, raining tears in defeat. There was nowhere else to run. The thing was everywhere.

And when the red cord of a tongue slithered out of the tunnel, she slapped at it feebly and whimpered, "Go back to hell."

It coiled around her neck and pulled her toward the door.

Somewhere on the brink of consciousness, Mercedes felt herself hit a floor and felt blood rush into her head and air into her lungs as her neck was freed—

—with a roaring that was not of a serpent or of any mortal creature, but a voice of legion, furious.

The wind, the angry wind.

5/2/225

The Ledges, New Africa, Southern, Aeolis

Draco looked so smug that Leader was certain the dragon had killed again. But Draco swaggered into the midst of the Outcast who were in the cave—Leader, Basilisk, Scorpii, and Vulpi—and announced, "The Ancient Ones talked to me."

"*You!*" Scorpii cried, and all the others reacted with sufficient astonishment to please Draco.

Ancient Ones. They were hard to conceive of—beings that existed ten thousand years in a world of nothing, not even hope. Old Ones could be grasped, but Ancient Ones were beyond comprehension—the closest things to deities the Kistraalians had. It was difficult to believe a being that made the Crossing could ever have been a creature like themselves.

And to be *talked* to by one . . .

"What did they say?" said Vulpi.

"They told me," Draco began with a giggle, "that if I did not leave that instant, I would have to sleep lightly for the rest of my life because as soon as my eyes were closed they would sweep up the nearest pointed object and drive it through my heart." He spoke glibly, but anyone could see that he was terrified.

Leader stared with his mouth open, then finally said, "What were you *doing*?"

"Just trying to feed my dragon," said Draco innocently.

"Feed it *who*?" Scorpii demanded, alarmed by Ancient Ones protecting Earthlings.

"An Earthling female. The police said she was a dancer."

"The Ancient Ones like dancers," said Leader, remembering the rafters full of Ancient Ones at the Gem Theater.

They must, thought Draco. *She spoke a few words of the ancient language.* Someone had been talking to her. But what could it portend?

5/2/225 Candle-in-the-Wind,

Drina Village, New Europe, Northern, Aeolis

Mercedes had crawled up the stairs to the dining room, gave up there, and fell into a semi-sleep sprawled on the floor.

It could only have been minutes when she heard a tube car coming up into the bay, and, suddenly regaining her strength, she ran to the cellar to make sure she had closed and locked the bay door. She saw the door ajar as the tube car came to a stop. She ran, slammed into the door with all her weight, and locked it with trembling hands.

Then she sank to her knees, bleating, waiting for the door to come crashing down.

But there came a soft knock and insistent voice. "Open."

"Niki!"

She opened the door, threw her arms around him, and cried, muffling shrieks of delayed hysteria against his chest, holding fast to his warm hard body. He held her awkwardly, as if he had never held anyone before. Niki made it a practice never to be touched. He would actually pull away from an attempted handshake, preferring to greet people with a bow—or a nod that approximated a bow. Unnerved by the sudden close contact now, he made the only involuntary action Mercedes had ever known him to do. He shivered.

Finally he took her shoulders and held her away from him.

"Monster," she bleated, still shaking, still terrified.

"They told me," said Niki. His maddening calm was soothing, and his powerful presence filled all the empty spaces, leaving little room for terror, as if his very being commanded a radius into which no one might step unpermitted, and monsters were forbidden. Then he said something so typical, so familiar, so innocently outrageous, that the horror left Mercedes' eyes and she laughed; he directed one of his quizzical plaintive looks at her and said, "Does this mean I can talk to you?"

"Yes," she said, laughing and still crying, trying to dry her tears. She tried to think of what to do now. "Should I call the Service?" she asked.

"No," said Niki. "They will just call you mad." He turned away, as if looking for something, nothing in particular, just something.

Mercedes sniffled, swallowed a few leftover sobs, then realized what he had just said. "Are you mad, Niki?" she asked.

"No," he said. "I just know too much."

A sense of wonder came over Mercedes. There was a reason. For everything. Niki's world was perfectly ordered. Insanity had no place in his scheme of things, and what seemed madness was merely an observer's ignorance and Niki's not bothering to justify himself to the ignorant.

What is it in your plan that I can't touch you?

"What are you looking for?" she asked, following his searching glance.

He turned to her. "Why it picked you. Eighty million square kilometers of land, a handful of Outcast monsters, and one picked you."

"The police said it was because I was alone." *That is a hint, Niki. That is a broad hint. That is an extremely rotund and obese hint—*

"Come stay with me," said Niki.

5/2/225

Thea Estate, Wilderness, Southern, Aeolis

Mercedes lay in a narrow bed in a small room beneath a slanted window that looked up the mountainside. She had fallen asleep watching three full moons rising over the summit.

She woke not much later while it was still night. Outside she could hear trees murmur, the sea rise, and waves thunder and crash. And she heard Niki. He came to her room, a trim silhouette in the door, and walked in softly.

He came to her bed, and she moved over. He knelt on the edge, leaned over her, and opened the window. He looked at the sky and trembled. "Not again," he murmured like a prayer. A breeze ruffled his hair.

"What is it?" Mercedes whispered.

Niki nodded at the sky.

The three moons had cleared the mountain and were so close together they were practically in line as they all moved into the shadow of the world.

"Eclipse," Mercedes said softly. She lay on her back and watched as the moons were all swallowed in shadow and turned a grotesque red.

She watched close to an hour, sometimes gazing at the moons, sometimes at Niki leaning over her, his hands on the sill, one knee on the bed, one foot on the floor, perfectly motionless but for an occasional blink and his slow imperceptible breathing.

"Niki, what's wrong?" she asked.

His lashes flickered, and he spoke, not really an answer, but like an echo of something told to him by a voice no one else could hear. "It can only get worse."

Chapter V.
Eclipse

5/2/225 Oasis Port,
Desert of the Bells, Northern, Aeolis

Luis Del Fuego hastened down the concourse to the hangar where the *Halcyon XLV* was berthed. He walked in the hatchway, which had been left open to the cool predawn air.

"Chief Del Fuego," Per Safir greeted him, as he tossed a dart into the board. "What do you have for us?"

"It is what you have for me, *capitán*," said the police chief. "Please hide me from these crazy people. Many many crazy people."

Per grinned. "Now what is this?"

"It is what is up there, *capitán*." He pointed to the sky.

"Oh, the eclipse," said Per. "I was watching it for a while."

The ascending and descending nodes of all three moons had intersected on the ecliptic, though the inclination of their individual orbital planes varied widely, from Kushuh's seventeen degrees, almost the same angle as the tilt of the planet on its axis, to the seventy degrees of the wayward boulder Taru, which, in some seasons, had a nearly circumpolar orbit. The moons now hung low above the southwest horizon, shrouded in bloody shadow.

"What's the trouble?" Per asked. "Seismic activity?"

"The quakes, they are not serious," said Del Fuego. "The people, they have seismic activity of the head. My phones do not rest, and on each one there is a madman. You must hide me, *capitán*. I do not want to answer the phones."

Per laughed. "Breakfast? Coffee?" he offered. He held up a dart. "Give me some competition?"

"I cannot eat before the sun comes up. I will take the coffee, but I cannot throw those things," said Del Fuego.

Per sighed, forced to compete against himself. He muttered, "Roxy is never around when you need her."

Buddy, who was standing on the ramp looking out toward the desert, piped up, "Chief, there go some of your crazy men." A group of stark-naked people were running out into the sand.

"No," said Del Fuego. "All the crazy men in the world are ringing my phones at this very moment. How can they be out there?"

"You missed some," Buddy said, watching the men chase desert lizards.

"Impossible. They are *all* on my phones. *My* phones."

"Is it pressure on the brain?" Per asked. "What is happening?"

"I do not know if the problem is physical or not," said the police chief. "The animals are crazy too. My horse, she threw me. My beautiful Andalusian mare—"

Per was taking aim as an eerie melody and a droning *thrum* wafted in with desert breeze. He let fly a wild toss that bounced off the bulkhead. *Thrum. Thrum. Thrum.* "Oh, my God, it's Roxanna's bagpipes come back to haunt me!" Per cried and dropped his remaining darts.

Buddy started to hoot as Del Fuego made to bolt from the cabin, no longer convinced of his host's sanity.

"Where is that horrible noise coming from?" Per bellowed and ran down the ramp, half-expecting to see the specter of a set of pipes with a Douglas tartan bag marching down the concourse of its own power.

What he saw, though, where a group of people had gathered, was a nobleman in a Sinclair tartan kilt, playing his own set of pipes, while the *Halcyon*'s first mate, Roxanna, danced over a pair of crossed swords in the middle of the concourse. She was splendidly cocky, and her step was spry and sure. Roxanna was not a classical beauty, but she had a smile that could light the night, and even the winds stopped to observe the dance and take in the strange music. The aristocrats standing by were smiling.

"They look at her like a performing seal," Per growled, arms crossed, noticing that because of the way the sound traveled, Roxanna's steps appeared out of sync at this distance.

"No, I think they like her," said Buddy. He was smiling.

It was near dawn and the eerie beautiful moons sank out of the world's shadow and touched the horizon.

On such a night as this the world had ended.

5/2/225 Remington Estate,
New Africa, Southern, Aeolis

At last the game made sense to East, why Laure seemed to enjoy inflicting pain. She took stabs at his heart to see if he bled—the only proof of affection she could demand of him. If the heart bleeds, it cares. She could not give love, only hurt. Pride, rank, and marital status precluded anything more. East wondered which of those obstacles was actually the one standing in her way. It had to be pride.

Caught with her emotions unveiled and vulnerable, Laure's temper was short, and she vented her anger on East simply for knowing.

"I ought to have you fired," she said, her voice strained.

East leaned in the doorway, his weight on one leg. "Maybe you ought to," he said quietly. *Who am I protecting you from? Why don't I go away?*

She narrowed her eyes as if he had insulted her. She was shaking in fury. "I don't think you can do your job," she said and ran outside into the night.

East did not know what she was up to. Normally she was more than capable of taking care of herself, but she was more distraught than ever he had seen her, so he ran after her and caught up with her in the garden.

She had stopped of her own accord in an open grove lit by the reflected shine of three full moons emerging from eclipse. Her face was tilted up toward his, her pupils dilated to make her eyes appear black. The night was cool, and East could sense her shivering. He put his jacket over her narrow shoulders—though there was no danger of her becoming ill—out of an instinct to protect, even if the lady did not need protecting. As his hand brushed her bare arm he felt her muscles tighten.

She looked into his eyes and said as if reading his mind, "What do you want to do to me?"

He had been thinking at that moment that he wanted to take her up in his arms, carry her to the house, and make love to her. He was so struck by the timing of her question that he could not speak.

She tossed back her dark hair and took his jacket from her shoulders. "Go ahead."

A seductress she was not. She was a hurt and jealous very young lady. East was certain she had never made love to anyone but her husband, which explained why, for all her sophistication, she was still naive and did not know the first thing about seducing anybody.

The very awkwardness of the attempt was painfully touching, and he would gladly have followed through, but through it all he still knew she was not herself.

He took her elbow with more authority than tenderness. "Come back to the house."

She jerked her arm out of his grasp and slapped him hard across the face. "I'll tell Stephen," she said.

"Tell him what?" he said in calm challenge.

"I'll tell him." Her voice went strident and her hands twisted East's jacket in agitation.

"I'm frightened," said East as gently as sarcasm would allow.

"You would do well to be," she said, and drew herself up imperiously, her shoulders stiff, head erect.

In reply he simply gazed into her eyes, which were wide, as in panic, his own eyes were calm slits of blue in wrinkled lids. Her lips, drawn tight and hard, began to quiver, and she dropped her gaze, threw East's jacket to the ground, and held her head between her hands as if it would burst under pressure from within.

East touched his hand to her chin and gently lifted her face to look at him, but she would not meet his eyes. She suddenly burst into tears, flung her arms around his waist more like a child than a woman, and cried, "Oh, East, what is happening to me!"

He embraced her, and his eyes turned up to the three sinister moons. He murmured, "High tide."

She cried in his arms, knowing she was stuck—little spider in a web of her own making. If it would have been any comfort, East could have told her that he was hopelessly tangled as well.

"Don't let go," she cried, her face against his chest.

He spoke almost too softly for her to hear. "Wouldn't think of it."

She was firm and warm, holding tight. He could feel her tremble against him, hear her breath, touch her hair. He hardened and knew she would feel it. *Dammit.* He couldn't help it.

She lifted her face from his chest and looked up. He looked back into her wild eyes and knew, just knew, she would do anything he asked.

And he didn't ask.

5/3/225 *Estate of the duchess Estelita,*

Little Asia, Northern, Aeolis

Leader let himself be dragged along with Scorpii, Basilisk, and Vulpi on a revel. The four of them walked unsteadily down the lane, wearing ill-fitting clothes, and passing a bottle of wine, which Leader thought tasted vile and felt worse, so he stayed most sober of the lot. He was also very nervous, recognizing where he was.

"The duchess's place is right over there." He pointed toward her mansion. He had been brought here when he had been caught by the Earthlings. And from here he had been taken to the place with the pit.

"Relax," said Scorpii. "We can be gone before anyone is sure they have seen us. Take one of these." She held out a handful of pills.

"What are they?" said Leader.

"Painkillers. They make you feel nice. An Earthman gave them to me."

"For what?"

"Services rendered," said Scorpii.

Leader blushed. "I mean, why? Are you in pain?"

"No." She laughed. "Take one."

"I don't want it," said Leader.

Basilisk did, and he swallowed one. Vulpi passed, preferring to stay with the wine.

Soon Basilisk began to smile, feeling the effect of the drug. "What else did that Earthman give you?" he asked Scorpii.

"Nothing," said Scorpii darkly, meaning that she was not pregnant. "There are no males on this planet. There are females and there are *tiqid*." She sneered the ancient word, not knowing its original reference to an infertile stage of a certain class of animals long extinct. She only knew the insult meaning which survived the Crossing.

Basilisk's smile vanished. "You are calling me a *tiqa*."

"I know I am," said Scorpii. "I haven't seen any results coming from you."

"Have you ever considered that the problem might be yours?" said Basilisk. "For all the times you have tried, *you* must be the *tiqa*."

"I am purebred. All I need is a male."

"I am right here," said Basilisk and grabbed her.

"No!" Scorpii protested.

"First time you ever said that," said Basilisk.

"I don't want to."

"Yes, you do. You want to be raped by my lizard, don't you?"

"Basilisk, stop it," Leader whispered.

Basilisk ignored him, taken with his idea. "Yes, I think you would like that. A big lizard with a webbed foot on your—"

"Quit it," Leader said, grimacing.

But Basilisk went on to describe it in the most revolting terms he could call to mind, then, becoming aroused by his own description, wrestled Scorpii to the ground, both of them trying to change form—he to lizard, she to wind—but they could not.

"Let me go!" Scorpii was screaming, clawing at him, as Leader and Vulpi tried to pull him off.

"If you don't want to, why aren't you gone?" Basilisk laughed.

"I *can't*!" Scorpii cried. "Get off!"

Then all four of them at once stopped pulling and lashing and screaming as the ground began to vibrate, but not from a quake.

Looming out of the dark very quickly—too quickly to think—came charging a team of twelve bolting black stallions shaking the earth with their great hoofs, their hairy fetlocks tossing, their moonstricken eyes rolling, and behind them rumbled a golden coach.

And suddenly it was upon them.

Vulpi and Leader vanished, their clothes falling empty under the hoofs.

Scorpii broke free of her startled attacker and dove into the bushes off the side of the path.

Basilisk froze, trying to change into wind and finding, astonished, that he could not.

And twelve sets of flying hoofs and the deep-gouging wheels of a golden coach charged down the lane.

When the thundering died in the distance, a voice bleated from the roadside. "Leader, help me."

Leader and Vulpi materialized. "Are you hurt?" said Leader.

"I can't change," Scorpii cried. "I can't change."

"Don't cry. As long as you are not hurt," said Leader, gasping, short of breath from horror at what lay in the road.

Scorpii crawled out of the bushes, scratched, her clothes torn. "Is he dead? I hope he is dead."

"He's dead," said Leader. He was forcing himself to think about a funeral when suddenly Vulpi roared, "*Robot!*"

A robot had come out of the ground, detecting something left on the horse path to be cleaned. But it stopped, detecting something wrong. It analyzed, checked the findings against its programming, and came out blank. This was something to be taken to the police. It began to gather up the remains of Basilisk.

"*Stay away!*" Vulpi screamed, picking up a log with which to smash the terrible machine.

"Leave it alone!" Scorpii ordered and grabbed at Vulpi's arms. "Let it go! He deserves it!"

"Stop! Stop! Stop!" Leader was trying to shout but his whispering voice was drowned out by the other two.

The fight ended when the robot disappeared into the ground, taking Basilisk with it. Vulpi and Scorpii froze where they were and stared at the blank space that was horrifyingly clean now.

And Vulpi vanished into the air, unwilling to remain at the site of the atrocity.

Scorpii turned to Leader, pleading. "He deserved it. You saw."

"I don't know," said Leader disjointedly. "I guess." Had Basilisk lived to see trial, the ring would have cast him out and declared him dead to its members, but Leader was too stunned and sickened to think about what was just and not just. "I don't know. It's over now."

A few drops of water splashed down from the sky, pattering on the ground and the forest leaves.

"Turn it off!" Scorpii cried, but that only worked when an Earthling lord or lady of high rank said it.

And it rained harder.

Scorpii had never been rained on in her life. She turned round eyes to Leader and begged, "Don't leave me here."

Leader shivered, naked, his skin raised rough all over with the chilling drops.

"Don't change form. Don't leave me by myself," said Scorpii, frightened to tears.

Leader stayed in humanoid form, and the two of them huddled close together, arms around each other, walking through the pelting rain.

"It is the pills," said Leader after a while, the realization coming to him. He did not explain the statement, but Scorpii knew what he was referring to.

The rain matted their hair, soaked Scorpii's clothes, and ran down their faces.

"Will I be trapped like this forever?" Scorpii wailed.

"Maybe it wears off, like alcohol," said Leader. He had a feeling she would be back to normal once the drug cleared from her system. After all, alcohol hangovers, though they felt like it, did not last forever. In time he was certain that Scorpii's inability to change form would be just a very sorry and expensive lesson learned.

But he would not like what she learned from it.

Chapter VI.
Dattas Setting

5/19/225 *Oasis Port,*

Desert of the Bells, Northern, Aeolis

Roxanna jogged up the ramp of *Halcyon,* brooding over her latest orders, and stopped short in the hatchway on seeing East inside the ship with Per and Buddy. "What is *he* doing here?" she said.

"Laure told me you had an order from the duchess," said East. "You don't mean to go through with it."

"We do," said Per.

"He does." Roxanna nodded at Per, wanting no part of the matter herself and glad that East obviously objected to it also. *Any ally in a war.*

Per Safir smiled at Roxanna. "Don't sound so negative. It may cure your hallucinations."

"If you mean my dragon, sir, I was not hallucinating any more than my jeep was," Roxanna snapped. "Nor my bagpipes. And I don't see how blowing up Dattas is going to get the Morts out of the desert—or explain away the *young* Mort."

Per scowled.

"What young Mort?" said East. All Morts found to date had been old, died presumably of old age.

"A robot brought in a young unidentified person. He—I *think* it was a he—had been trampled by horses—the duchess's own horses, to judge from the size of the hoofprints," said Roxanna.

"What did you find out from it?" East asked.

"From the Mort? Nothing." Roxanna smiled sourly. "The police annihilated it."

"What?"

"It was making them ill," Roxanna explained.

Squeamish police. What next? "The duchess's horses trample a young man to death and now La Estelita is going to solve everything by having one of the moons blown up. That makes a whole lot of sense," East said.

"But you can't argue that spring tide wasn't a twenty-megaton headache this last time with all three moons pulling on us," Per argued.

It certainly was, thought East.

"Dattas was scheduled for destruction two hundred years ago by the surveyors," Per continued. "They knew it would give us trouble in time, but it was kept because the sight of three moons was too pretty to give up."

"But now that all three moons aren't due to stack up again for a good long time, what is the hurry?—other than to take some political pressure off Estelita and make it look as if she is doing something," said Roxanna.

"An order is an order," said Per.

"But you really don't mind this one."

"No. I always wanted to do this," Per admitted. "Is there a spaceman alive who hasn't fantasized about blowing up a world?"

"A moon."

"Close enough. Wouldn't any ship captain give his eyeteeth for this chance?"

"The megalomaniacal ones, I suppose," said Roxanna.

East put on his hat.

"Leaving already?" said Per.

"I have to be back at Southern before dawn and La Laure wakes up," said East.

"That woman walks all over you, East," said Roxanna. "I admit it's entertaining to watch, but I can't understand why you put up with it."

"Roxanna, if I were you I would be very grateful that there are people in this galaxy who put up with obnoxious young women," said East. He nodded a farewell and left, Per accompanying him.

A half-dozen responses occurred to Roxanna minutes later. She told them all to Buddy. He made her settle down to a chess game, but after a while she was still muttering. "I've taken as much aggravation as I can bear. Not just from them.

This whole world. Aeolians make me feel this big." She held up a pawn, practically the only piece she had left on the board. "It's not even that they are so much richer than I am, or so much more cultured, or so much prettier, or even that they have enough land to feed a million buffalo. It's their five-light-year-long names that I can't stand." Roxanna was adopted and did not have a name that was *really* her own. Douglas she waved like a banner.

"Well, look at Per," said Buddy. "Safir is just his mother's name translated into Swedish. Per's mother was a space-station prostitute named Sapphire."

"Even so, it's *his* name," said Roxanna. She leaned forward and spoke as if revealing her darkest secret. "Buddy, I'm not even sure I'm Scottish."

"You probably are. The UBC is good at matching up adoptees and parents. And don't worry about the name; only dogs need pedigrees."

"Thanks, Buddy," said Roxanna.

"Anytime. Check. You're not concentrating."

"No, I'm not," said Roxanna. "I've been thinking about—everything—the Morts, my dragon, the marquise, this." She put a finger on her horselike figurine, which she had been using for a knight on the chessboard. Then she picked up her king, took it out of check, and moved it across the board in a blatantly illegal move. "What would you say if I moved from here to here?"

"I'd say you were cheating," said Buddy.

Roxanna met his eyes across the board. "Buddy, somebody's cheating." She was not talking about chess.

Buddy picked up her horse figurine and turned it over in his hands. He nodded, "Either that or . . ."

"Or?"

"Maybe we don't know the rules."

5/20/225

New Europe, Northern, Aeolis

A crow atop the highest branch of the tallest bare tree, a solitary sentry, cawed twice, three times, then spread its wings to the winds of coming winter and abandoned its barren perch with slow wingbeats, its warning call echoed by others, and all the birds foraging on the ground amid the gravestones took flight with chatters, clicks, and whistles, and they perched in the evergreens. Themselves hidden, the voices of many disturbed creatures calling to each other yet remained.

The Outcast came up the walk. Fallen leaves like spies betrayed his passage, and bubbling chirping voices conveyed the word through the evergreens.

This was the graveyard of the earliest Earthling dwellers on the planet, not the aristocracy, but the builders and surveyors, who were rewarded with one of the most precious of all possessions, a piece of land as a resting place for all time.

The grounds were unkempt, the place forgotten. The brick walls were overgrown, the clustered graves covered with fallen leaves and brown-yellow grass, the stones weathered. Ivy that had outgrown its original urn spilled out and strangled the adjacent markers. No one took care of this place, only the wilderness robots, which tended it like a forest. The wilderness crept in, and carrion was left for the crows. Commoners had ceased being buried on Aeolis two hundred years ago. No one came here anymore.

Yet, off behind some evergreens, in a shallow vale where no paths led and no markers were, like a private sector still within the cemetery, the Outcast was startled to see a burial taking place.

The Outcast huddled into a hollow formed by the roots of a great gnarled tree to hide and watch.

The grave was not dug down, but instead dug into the side of the embankment, without a vault, just a horizontal shaft. The coffin was placed inside, then covered over without a facing stone, without a marker, without a trace, the sod replaced to cover the wound in the hillside.

Then the gravediggers planted a small evergreen, and they left, shaking their heads, not comprehending their job, leaving behind a lone mourner, who crossed his arms, fists upon opposite shoulders, and bowed his head, a look of held-back pain in his dark eyes.

Then he lifted his head, dropped his hands to his sides, and stood a moment. He walked to the new little tree and spat on the ground at its base, but not in the contemptuous way that Earthlings usually used the gesture, and then he too left, but with slow measured steps.

And the wind moaned.

5/20/225 Ledges,

New Africa, Southern, Aeolis

Night. Several of the Outcast had gathered in a ring, not for any ritual, but to draw silent comfort from each other's presence.

A soft thud of a small metal bar falling onto the pressed dirt outside the ring made them all turn and look as Vulpi materialized out of the air. He stooped to pick up the bar, which he had spirited there on his wind form. Though small, the metal piece had some weight, and it would have taken a great deal of effort to carry as wind, so it had to have some importance.

Vulpi gave it to Leader. "What does that say?"

It took Leader's feeble eyes a moment to focus on the incised pattern of markings smudged with dirt. Then his hands began to tremble and he nearly dropped the bar. The pattern was printing in the ancient language. "It's someone's *name*," Leader whispered in awe.

The other Outcast in the ring leaned forward to look, but Leader covered the bar with his hands. None of them had any right to look upon this.

"Where did you get this?" said Leader.

"Under a tree," said Vulpi.

"But it's *new*," said Leader in disbelief. These bars were usually made out of iron and rusted quickly. This one had not even oxidized.

"It was in the tree roots when I saw it planted," said Vulpi.

Leader stood up. "Show me where."

"What are you going to do with it?" said Vulpi.

"Take it back," said Leader. "*Now*."

5/20/225

New Europe, Northern, Aeolis

The Outcast rematerialized in the graveyard, where night had fallen and the only light was the half-glow of Dattas and Taru.

"The trees. Look at them," said Scorpii.

Because of the varied sizes and the interspersal of chance-sown deciduous trees, it was not readily apparent, but the evergreens formed a very wide circle—a ring.

And one tree in the ring was a little pine sapling uprooted. Leader took the metal bar he carried, placed it among the pine's roots, and gently replanted the little tree. He could not understand how Vulpi could be so appalled at what had happened to Basilisk, then turn around and dig up a name.

Vulpi was standing by the embankment. "This is where the body is."

"What does it mean?" Little Bird asked Leader, who was still crouching by the tree.

"This is how they used to bury the dead before the Crossing," said Leader with awestruck reverence. "They stopped doing it after the Crossing because the robots would dig them up. That's when we started burning our dead."

"Why doesn't a robot dig this one up?" said Little Bird.

"Because it is an Earthling grave. The Earthling who owns the land tells the robots that there is supposed to be a dead person here, so the robots leave it alone."

Draco was prowling among the trees. "Who did this?"

"A man," said Vulpi. "He did a *shanai* over the grave." He crossed his arms, fists on shoulders.

"Look at all these trees," said Scorpii. Each one would hold the name of an Ancient One or an Old One. "Why would an Earthling bury a Kistraalian in his precious land—with a Kistraalian rite?"

"I wish I knew," said Leader.

"Could he be one of ours?" Pega suggested.

"And own land? He would have to have an Earthling ID. They have a machine that knows everyone," said Leader. "I don't see how."

"Then it *is* an Earthman," said Scorpii. "Leader, they are taking over the world."

"They *have* taken it over," said Leader resignedly.

Draco bristled. "Treat Earthlings like people," he growled. "They don't even belong here. They are animal fodder."

Suddenly a flash like thunderless lightning made them all look up to see the moon Dattas glow like a supernova, then disintegrate before their eyes. Some of them screamed.

"See what they do!" said Draco. "They take and take and take and they destroy and rearrange, and the Ancient Ones treat them like . . ." He lost voice in outrage. His mind shifted to thoughts of revenge. He knew how. And he knew who. The little dancer was gone from Candle-in-the-Wind, but he knew someone better. "Some kind of native," he said.

Her time was overdue.

5/20/225

New Africa, Southern, Aeolis

East had been a little surprised and angry at himself for not taking advantage of the situation in the garden, for he had never been one for heeding someone else's marriage vows. But none of that was really the point. He wanted to own Laure, not borrow her for an evening. He would not have been able to give her back.

Once the tides evened out and Laure was back to normal, East could not begin to guess if she would be angry or grateful that one of them had stayed in control.

She was both. And she still had not forgiven him for knowing what she felt—which was to say she had not forgiven herself for dropping her guard.

"You wanted me," she said accusingly.

"Very badly," said East, making no attempt to deny or explain.

The reply disarmed her, and left her too startled to make further comment. She let it go at that for several days, troubled, at war with herself. And when she had East pilot her ship out to the desert beyond the Ledges so she could watch the destruction of the moon Dattas, she made her husband come with her. She hung on Stephen's arm fiercely, as if for her life. *This is my husband*, her actions screamed, too emphatically. *I love him. I do. Really.*

Once arrived at the desert, though, she left his side, for Stephen preferred to remain inside the ship. He hated the outdoors.

Laure and East went outside.

The ship *Windhover* rested on a flat plain of sand beneath a night sky that seemed twice as black as any in the world. The waning moon Dattas reached its zenith in the black sky, then it exploded in a glowing fireball. Laure watched till the blackness reclaimed the sky, turning it darker than before.

East turned the ship lights back on. He felt uneasy, for no reason—for no *good* reason. He had heard a whistling in the dark, which his father would say meant that a ghost was near.

But there was only Laure, dressed in flowing white like a specter in the desert wind.

Then the wind picked up. "Ah. *Simoun*," said Laure, closing her eyes. She drew a veil across her face to keep out the dust.

Then the serpent rose out of the sand.

Before his brain could even form the word *impossible*, East had run clear of the ship to draw the serpent's attention away from Laure.

But the beast was not interested in him and only looked his way when Laure ran to his side. East roughly shoved Laure behind him and pushed her to the ground.

The enormous reptilian head swayed on its long coiling body, blinkless eyes glowing green.

Roxanna's dragon.

It roared—as serpents did not—and opened its jaws to consume both of them.

The hunter in East balked at killing a rare animal—but not when it was stalking Laure. Where, East wondered in a split second, does one shoot a monster to kill it, not wound it? He could not afford to risk enraging an already wounded animal—one coil of the beast looked as if it had been hit by a truck. One chance. It had to be good. The lady was watching.

He fired into its gaping mouth, a voice in the back of his mind reminding him that it was bad luck to kill snakes.

The serpent's head bolted straight up, rising the entire length of its body, then fell over stiffly like a tower, and lay dead on the ground.

Lord Stephen ran out of the ship and stumbled across the soft ground to help his wife to her feet. He was shaking. She was not.

East walked to the serpent to make sure of his kill. He fired two more shots into its head. *Well, Father, what do you have to say about this?*

Father would probably hope that the amount of bad luck had nothing to do with the size of the snake.

Laure brushed off the dust and sand that clung to her

dress, and ran lightly to East and threw her arms about his neck. "You were wonderful." She kissed his cheek.

East did not look at her, only felt her arms around him, kept a stoic expression, and stared off past his kill, enjoying the realization of a very old forgotten fantasy. Hell, it was even sort of a dragon, and almost a princess.

Lord Stephen Remington, who was not in the fantasy, broke the moment by marching up and vigorously shaking East's hand, thanking him for saving his wife. Why did Stephen have to call her "his wife"? Why couldn't he have just called her Laure? The man did not even seem to mind that "his wife" had her arms around East's neck. Maybe the lord was so confident of Laure's fidelity that it did not matter, but he could at least have looked a little concerned.

To the lord's profuse thank-you's East said only, "It's what you're paying me for."

"Mercenaries," said Laure. "Isn't he terrible?" She was smiling.

Lord Remington tried to lead his wife away from the horrible serpent's corpse, but Laure walked around it once to see what East had killed for her.

East went back to the ship *Windhover* to radio Commander Roxanna Douglas, who had stayed behind at Oasis while the *Halcyon* destroyed the moon Dattas. East told her he had a surprise for her if she would come out immediately, and he gave her the location. She reluctantly agreed to come.

Roxanna arrived in a police shuttle. She jumped out of the cockpit and gave a terrific yell to the desert night. She slapped her knees and circled the beast, repeating despite herself, "Oh, East. Oh, *East!*" She pointed with glee at the bloody impressions on one side of the scaled body. "Look. Those are my dents. That's my jeep! You can see the headlights!" She clapped her hands and skipped to East. "East, East, *East*, you've saved my career!" She grasped either lapel of his jacket, laughing close to crying. "They all had me thinking I was crazy. You can see the dents from my jeep! Thank you, East!"

"I thought you'd like it," said East. "I have to take my clients home," he said, nodding at the lord—and the lady, who was watching like a hawk. "I trust you can take care of this from here, Commander."

"Yes," she said, still laughing.

And when *Windhover* took off, Roxanna was left alone in the desert, she and the serpent casting long stark shadows in the cold floodlights of her transport. She became solemn, still elated but more quietly, remembering someone else who should have been here but was not.

Marquise Des Vaux, I hope you can see this.

5/21/225 Oasis Port,
Desert of the Bells, Northern, Aeolis

The *Halcyon* did not take long to clear screening at Kushuh, proceeding directly to the final station and, being pronounced still clean, returned to Aeolis in a matter of hours.

Roxanna was waiting with a jeep to take Per to see something.

"Where are we going?" said Per, who hated surprises.

"The other side of the port," said Roxanna.

"What have you come up with now?"

"It's a Mort—after a fashion," said Roxanna. "Anyway, it's dead and the UBC has no identification for it."

She stopped the jeep at their destination.

Per frowned. "This is a meat importhouse, Roxy. How revolting."

"It was the only place equipped to handle something this size," she said, getting out of the jeep.

"Awfully big Mort," Per said, following her.

"I'll say," said Roxanna.

Per was looking at his feet when he walked into the storage room. He almost stepped on what looked like a length of oddly textured red cord. He bent down and picked it up. "What the hell is this doing here—someone could trip—"

He looked up at Roxanna and found himself eyeball to eyeball with a serpent as big as a tree. "Roxy, that's a—"

Then he noticed, protruding from the serpent's mouth, a long red cord of a tongue that extended across the floor and—

"Gagh!" Per jumped back, dropping the tongue, then stared at Roxanna, stock still, round-eyed and speechless.

Roxanna stared back, leaned against the dragon, and said, "I told you so."

5/22/225 Oasis Port,

Desert of the Bells, Northern, Aeolis

The crew of the *Halcyon* sent off a biopsy of the serpent to their superiors for analysis, hoping to get a clue of what kind of planet the creature might be from, for, though the serpent was unquestionably alien to Earth, it was not necessarily a returning native of Aeolis.

Then East came by the ship. "Gotten a report on that thing yet?" he asked.

"Still waiting," said Roxanna.

East's gaze fell on the chessboard, where Roxanna's horse-like figurine stood. He picked it up. It seemed familiar, though it was nothing he had ever seen before. Then he remembered.

How did you get through the forest?

I rode a wild horse. She's very shy. She's pure white and slender as a unicorn. Her hoofs are silver and cleft, she has a lion's mane, and she runs fast as the wind.

He put the horse down. He did not know where the figurine had come from and assumed it was a likeness someone had made recently on sighting the "impossible" creature. "I guess we have to believe this is real too," he muttered.

With great effort, Buddy spoke casually. "You've seen a creature like that?"

"Laure did," said East, and put on his hat and left.

And Buddy stared after him.

"Buddy, what is it?" said Roxanna.

"Roxanna—your horse. It's over ten thousand years old, right? It has to represent a native, right?"

"Oh, my God," said Roxanna, suddenly seeing the implication. "If Lady Laure Remington saw a live one—"

"Then she must have seen a native," Per finished for her. "Roxy, you were right."

"I don't want to be right!" she cried. If she was right, Earth might stand to lose the whole world.

"Don't panic until we're sure," said Per. "And even then don't panic. It's not necessarily the end of the world. Any beings who abandon a planet for ten thousand years can be said to have given up their claim on it, and are going to have a hard time proving they have a right to take it back."

"Shall I catch up with East to make sure?" Roxanna offered, starting out the hatchway.

"*No!*" said Per, and Roxanna froze. "Don't get him suspicious."

"*Suspicious?*" Roxanna said, growing frightened. "Why?"

"If there really are returning natives, there are going to be people who automatically assume it means the loss of their land, and they will try to suppress the evidence—ourselves included in that evidence. So don't breathe the possibility to anyone."

"Not even East?" said Roxanna.

"Not even East. If it came down to a choice, I think he'd sell out to the pretty lady."

5/22/225 Thea Estate,
Wilderness, Southern, Aeolis

With the dragon dead, Mercedes moved back to Candle-in-the-Wind, for Niki was very possessive of his solitude. She was wandering through one of the ghost-designed rooms of Niki's mansion on her last day there when her eye was caught by a piece of parchment. She picked it up. It was an envelope addressed to Niki in gold print. On the back was the duchess's seal. "Niki, what is this?"

"I don't know," said Niki with a total lack of interest.

"Can I open it?" said Mercedes.

"If you like."

It was an invitation to the duchess's soirée two days hence. The invitation was dated much much earlier. "Niki, you must accept right away."

"I am not going to accept at all," said Niki.

"Oh, no, Niki, you mustn't turn her down. Her wrath is never-ending."

"Duchesses come and duchesses go. I shall survive her wrath."

"How can you say that? Duchesses come and duchesses stay. The last one reigned here sixty years. This one has been here all my life—"

"Which is only a moment."

"Thank you," said Mercedes, who, like most dancers, panicked about aging. "But you have to go."

"I cannot afford to waste the time. A few vain breaths and

123

suddenly you are old. Moments fly. I shan't spend them on the duchess."

Mercedes held her silence. She had never met anyone so time-conscious. His heart did not beat, it ticked, and he lived with an urgency, as if he had only a short time left. But time was relative, and to what, she wondered, was he comparing his days of mortality that they seemed so brief?

5/22/225 Drina Village,

New Europe, Northern, Aeolis

"That is the man!" Vulpi pointed.

Leader shrank in fear at the sudden outcry. "What man?" He immediately thought of the one who had killed Draco. When Draco had not returned to boast of his kill, Leader had sent out Leo to see what had happened. Leo reported that a man had shot the dragon and that the Service was holding its body. "What man? Where?"

"The one I saw who has been burying Kistraalians," said Vulpi. He made no effort to conceal himself, for he was pointing not at a living man but at a hologram.

Leader stared in amazement at the image of a pair of dancers—a lovely woman up on point, and the man standing before her, looking into her eyes.

"Do you think . . . ?" Vulpi ventured.

A man who danced for Ancient Ones and Old Ones. A man who disappeared without a trace for years at a time and reappeared unchanged. A man so different from others that he was called mad.

Leader whispered, skin tingling, mind overwhelmed, *"He has got to be one of us!"*

5/22/225 Cave of the Winds,

The Ledges, New Africa, Southern, Aeolis

"Niki Thea?" Scorpii echoed, staring at Vulpi across the subterranean pool in the Cave of the Winds.

Most of the Outcast had gathered there since Draco's death, looking for strength in each other.

"A Kistraalian," said Vulpi. "For what it is worth."

"But Niki is an Earthman," said Pega. "He came on an Earthship. He has an Earth ID."

"Perhaps he came from Earth," said Scorpii. "But that does not make him an Earthman. It would just mean his parents stowed away on an Earthship and he was born on Earth."

"Why would anyone do that?" said Pega. "They say Earth is not as pretty as Aeolis."

"But Aeolis used to be desolate. There was no way to survive in physical form in the early days after the Crossing," said Scorpii. "Isn't that right, Leader?"

"That is before my time," said Leader, who was only a hundred years old—and even that seemed an eternity. "He would have to be very old."

"But if he is one of us, why doesn't he tell us?" said Pega.

"He is not an Outcast," said Leader. "He would not talk to us."

"Then why bother?" said Vulpi, throwing a pebble into the pool.

"Vulpi," Scorpii said, leaning over the stone pool, "I want a baby."

Vulpi dropped another pebble into the water. He had heard this many times before. "Do you think he can?"

Tauri, who had given up long ago, suddenly revived her hope and said, "If he is not Outcast, *of course he can!*" One could not be a mule and yet not be an Outcast, for sterility was a crime of being.

All the females began to stir and exchange looks of guarded hope.

"But they say he is a recluse and he hates women," said Leo. Making children was not an activity Leo considered civilized, and it would not do for his hero to be involved in such things.

"Recluse! Nonsense," said Scorpii. "He's *wind*—that is why no one ever sees him. And as for hating women, of course he would not consort with Earthwomen—the Ancient Ones would cast him out for that."

"They will also cast him out if he consorts with you," said Vulpi.

"Vulpi, you are not helping," said Scorpii.

"You don't need my help. If you all want children, why don't you get together and gang-rape him?"

"That is not funny," said Scorpii.

And the more she thought about it, the less funny it was.

5/23/225 Drina Village,

New Europe, Northern, Aeolis

Niki was skittish descending the steps, staying close to Mercedes's side. It had become impossible for the two of them to leave the theater without people crowding around to talk to them, take their picture, and record for off-planet releases what they said, what they wore, what they did, for they were a pretty pair, the darlings of Aeolian society.

They shrank from the cameras and the questions, and ran to the dark tree-canopied lane.

Too sudden to know why, Niki's foot jackknifed inward, and he went down. He landed, startled, on his right hip, the offending ankle in front of him. On his face was a look of surprise, then bewilderment. Stumbling was alien to Niki. After a stunned instant he felt the pain.

Mercedes knelt down. "Oh, my God, Niki," She put her arms around him, and this time he did not draw away.

The crowd of people caught up with them, and hologramic cameras hemmed them in. Niki hid his face in Mercedes's encircling arms, shying from the cameras and crowd. People were shoving to get a picture of the ballerina comforting the fallen Niki.

A doctor tried to come near, but Niki leaned protectively over his ankle and barked at the man not to touch him.

Long after the cameras and gawkers were chased away, Niki still sat there in Mercedes' arms, just waiting, refusing to be carried or to call for a carriage.

It was very dark and quiet again. Niki rested his head against Mercedes. She could feel his lashes on her collarbone and expected any moment to feel tears, but he did not cry, remaining in quiet, stoic shock.

Mercedes stayed with him, growing cold despite his nearness, listening to the wind in the trees, the crickets, and the voice of a nightingale, and watching the ghostly lights of fireflies.

A rabbit hopped out of the ferns—not a real one, for there were no rabbits on Aeolis, but a robot, sniffing them for alcohol. It was programmed to summon a carriage for drunks in public places. Satisfied, it retreated into a thicket.

Tentatively, Niki moved his foot, and breathed a prayer of thanks to a god he did not believe in to find his ankle only sprained, not broken.

He did not mention any plan either to have a doctor repair it or to cancel the performance the day after tomorrow. He merely said, "I may as well attend the duchess's nonsensical gathering. There is not much else I can do."

5/24/225 Remington Estate,
New Africa, Southern, Aeolis

Stephen Remington had bowed out of attending the duchess's soiree, which was likely to be more like a grand ball, for he was unsure of himself, afraid of saying or doing something unforgiveable, like choosing the wrong wine, stepping on his dance partner's foot, forgetting someone's name, using the wrong fork, eating the wrong thing with his fingers, or spilling something.

So Laure chose for her escort her bodyguard, East, who was ashamed of nothing and awkward in no situation. He neither followed the rules nor broke them, for he was outside of them. Rules did not apply to his kind.

Laure's father, Lord LaFayette, looked askance at her choice and voiced doubt as to the propriety, but Laure said, "It is as proper as taking you, Daddy. East saved my life, and he shot that awful monster. I am sure the duchess's friends would love to meet him."

Lord LaFayette could not dispute what she said and was forced to concede that, though unconventional, there was nothing outwardly improper about it. He only wished that she had asked someone else—anyone else—because Lord LaFayette had been around long enough to see how his daughter looked at her bodyguard and how East looked at his daughter.

"Besides, I've made up my mind," said Laure. "Find him something to wear, Daddy."

Lord LaFayette sighed and set about the impossible task of making East look presentable.

Laure herself wore flowing white ornamented with yards of pearls in her headdress, on her belt, and hanging like teardrops on the edge of her shawl. When she heard a knock on her door and her father's voice—"It is the best I could do, *chérie*; you did not give me much to work with"—she rose from her dressing table, opened the door, and cried, "East, you look handsome!"

"I would not say *that*," Lord LaFayette grumbled.

He was certainly striking, in shades of gray and pale blue that seemed to intensify his thick silver hair and the piercing blue of his eyes. His hair had been trimmed but retained an untamed silver brush at the back of his neck like a wolf's ruff. Aeolians were fastidious about the backs of their necks, but here East drew the line.

"He looks like a savage in civilized clothing," Lord LaFayette groaned.

"He is," said Laure to a wink from East. She stood beside East, took his arm, and asked her father, "Do we match?"

"Most definitely not."

They did. Perfectly.

5/24/225 *Estate of the duchess Estelita*

Little Asia, Northern, Aeolis

On arriving at the duchess's estate in the ship *Windhover*, Laure and East were met at the garden's edge by the duchess's coach drawn by twelve black stallions, the high-stepping breed developed from Shires and Clydesdales, with an abundance of feather over their huge hoofs, and standing a massive twenty-two hands high. "The duchess's stallions," Laure said, nodding at them. "And the duchess's stallions." She nodded at the two musclebound footmen—with expansive chests, broad shoulders, blond curls, and pouting full lips—who opened the door of the coach for Laure and her escort, and drove them to Estelita's palace.

There, two more minions opened the gates for them, and another took Laure's gold card inside and announced them. A wide flight of carpeted steps brought them through a gilded archway into the high-domed ballroom, big enough to swallow a freighter, with lofty coffered ceiling, muraled and pilastered walls, a raised dais for an orchestra, and a floor so black it reflected no light and seemed to extend downward to infinity. White doves glided in the dome and perched and billed on the crystal chandeliers. *Holograms,* thought East, for no one was ducking.

East created a minor stir on his entrance with Laure. He was too rugged, too dangerous, too real, and too ugly. Yet, as the man who had slain the dragon, he was treated with the most deference the Aeolians ever showed to a commoner.

East considered them with more or less tolerant contempt. Rich men kissed each other in greeting; men did not kiss in the part of Arizona East was from. And the rich held onto each other in a way he could not abide, as if, were even one to stand alone, they would all tumble like a house of cards.

A woman who should have been beautiful approached Laure. Physically the woman was flawless, but she walked like a barge, too far forward, too stiff-legged, her head too haughty, her large bosom thrust out like a rutting city pigeon. Her gown was red and black velvet and satin, and her blond hair was ornamented with a large ruby aigrette. Her face, though young in features, was pinched, frowning, with too red lips.

Old, struck East. An old crone in a many-times-rejuvenated body. East could tell he was in the presence of his elder.

She tapped East with her walking stick, then held its diamond hilt under his chin, inspecting his face. "Gladiator, Laure?" she said.

"No, ma'am. Bodyguard," said Lady Laure.

"Pity. He would be a good one. Not too brawny. A little thin, but then it is the tough lean ones that are always the best. Those slabs of beef are beautiful but they never last long."

"No, ma'am."

When the woman was out of earshot once again, East asked, "Who the hell is she?"

"Who is She," said Laure. "Say that with a capital, Mr. East. She is the duchess Estelita. If Aeolis ever becomes an independent monarchy, she will be our queen."

"In the meantime, she's your battleship."

Laure giggled. "Don't be so flip."

"She hates you," said East.

"She does," said Laure. "News reporters have a habit of calling me the First Lady of Aeolis because of my birth. Of course, that is her title, and she will never let me forget it."

East was watching where Estelita had gone. His attention was caught by the man she had accosted, definitely not the typical Aeolian. He was too short, too young, too strong, and no Aeolian ever limped—at the slightest scratch they all went running to their doctors. He was accompanied by an equally unusual young woman, slight of frame, gazellelike, with immense misty brown eyes—a chaste beauty with a girlish figure.

"Niki Thea and Mercedes Stokolska," said Laure, seeing where his gaze led.

Together the dancers looked like a pair of charming innocents—confronted by a dragon.

When the duchess moved on, Laure took East by the hand and said, "Come. I want to meet Niki. The man is a legend."

She walked up to the dancer to introduce herself, but, before she could, Niki bowed and said, "You are Laure Eva Aeolia LaFayette."

The names of hers that he omitted—one in particular—did not distress East at all.

"How did you know that?" Laure smiled.

"I was told," said Niki, then looked at East. "Who is this?"

"His name is East," said Laure.

"East what? What East?" said Niki, slightly irritated and impatient.

"None of your business," said East.

Niki's reaction was unexpected. His demeanor changed, his eyes livened, interest sparked. "Why?" he asked, not at all casually.

East smiled wryly. "The Navaho believe names are powers. You use it when you need it, so you don't wear it out."

"You are one of these Navaho?"

"My father thinks he is, and he gave me the name."

"Niki is not my real name," said Niki, and Mercedes's eyes widened in surprise. "Neither is Thea. I never use my real name."

East cocked his head. "Why? You're not a Navaho."

"It has always been that way. I do not know why. I wonder sometimes. Does it give you strength really?"

East shrugged.

"I would like to know," said Niki.

At this point, some aristocrats who had collected to listen dived into the conversation and took off on a philosophical tack. East shut up and let Niki deal with them—and began to notice the dancer's incredible composure. He saw in the smooth unlined face not a lack of years or lack of experience, or even lack of emotion, but an impenetrable wall of defense drilled to perfection, prepared for anything. His control was more than human. It took a chaos of mind to worship discipline so.

What the hell have you been through this side of hell to be the way you are?

Niki was responding to someone's statement with one of his dogmatic assertions to which he would brook no argument. "Everyone is fundamentally evil. The good merely lack opportunity."

East was not a philosopher, but he could not let that one slide by. "This may make you gag, but I consider myself good," said East. "Opportunity has nothing to do with it. If a chance isn't there it can be made."

Niki turned to him the eyes of a sphinx and, instead of defending, said very quietly, "I shall remember you said that."

5/24/225 *Cave of the Winds,*

The Ledges, New Africa, Southern, Aeolis

"I found Niki's house," said Scorpii to the circle of frantically hopeful faces surrounding her in the cave. "He was away but there were Ancient Ones and Old Ones everywhere. I escaped before someone could realize what I was. If a few of you can draw them off for a moment, the rest of us can slip into Niki's room and lock the winds out. We can be done and out before any of them find out what is happening and blow the door down—or get through the door—some of them can do that."

Leader was staring at her. "What can you be talking about?"

"You know," said Scorpii.

"No, I don't."

"Children."

Tauri spoke. "What is to keep Niki in humanoid form for this?"

"He is in pain," Scorpii began.

Leader choked.

"I saw painkillers by his bed. He will be dancing tomorrow night. He will have to be in agony afterward. He will take a pill and go to sleep. That is our time."

"I have a question," said Little Bird timidly. "How do we make him . . . well . . . cooperate?"

"MCR, if he is unwilling," Scorpii said and held out a drug injector—filled. MCR was very hard to find because it was illegal and unimportable, and so had to be processed on-planet. "I had to steal this from the duchess."

Leader, who had been standing outside the circle, dumbstruck, finally managed to sputter, "This is . . ." and he could not find a word. "You cannot do this."

Scorpii glared at him. "You said you would do everything in your power to give me a child. This is the last chance for our kind."

"If this is what it takes, maybe it is not worth saving."

"If it were within you to beget, you would understand," said Scorpii. "If Kistraal dies it will not be my fault."

"You do not even know if this will save our people or prolong our death. You have no idea what Niki's animal form is. All your offspring could be mules."

"I have an idea what he is," said Scorpii. "No one has sighted an animal of a different caste from any of ours—so his animal must be identical to one of ours and we have been mistaking him for one of us all this time."

"Maybe," said Leader. "But even if he is of the scorpion caste and you did have a child, Scorpii, who is that child going to mate with? The only way this abomination has a chance of saving us is if Niki's animal is a white dog like the Pleiades. Otherwise this is all for nothing, and, Scorpii, you have no right!" He was screaming at her in his whispery voice. Scorpii was speechless. "You would destroy the only good we have left. He is the only one of us with a reason to live."

"Then let him perpetuate his kind!" Scorpii lashed back.

Leader saw in her fury what exactly he was facing. He had heard that the will to survive was the strongest. How much stronger then was the will of a species to preserve itself. "I forbid this," said Leader.

"Then, Leader, this is a mutiny."

5/24/225 *Estate of the duchess Estelita,*

Little Asia, Northern, Aeolis

East had separated himself from the others to search for a beer, which was not forthcoming. Then he heard a voice at his elbow. "Sir, are there any more dragons?"

His first impulse was to snap, "Now how the hell would I know that?" But something told him to look first to see who asked, for it had been a timid light voice speaking German, and she had called him "Sir." He looked to his side, then down. It was the little dancer, Mercedes. East choked on his retort. He would sooner step on a ladybug. He looked into her dark frightened eyes and knew at once that she had seen the thing.

"I don't know," he said. "I wish I could tell you. I just know there's one less than there was."

She paused a second, stood up on tiptoe, kissed his cheek, and fled, leaving East feeling startled, warm, and silly. That one made him feel like a grandfather too, but he did not mind at all.

He turned around again, and there was the duchess Estelita. All tender feelings scattered.

"You are a Service veteran," said Estelita.

You've done some fast checking, haven't you, lady? thought East. Then, *Why?* "I am," said East.

"Then perhaps you can tell me what those worthless Service officers that have taken root on my planet have been doing all this time."

"Having great difficulty," East answered. "I hear your horses ran down some evidence, but the police threw it out."

The duchess was not pleased. "What of the dragon? Where do they claim it is from?"

Claim? "They don't claim anything. They don't know."

"Surely they have an idea."

"No."

"Hiding it, are they?" said Estelita.

That never occurred to East. "What have they to hide?"

"What have you?" She narrowed her eyes at him. "Besides murder."

"That is an open record," said East.

"Are all Service officers criminals?"

"Not the officers," said East. "So don't worry about the *Halcyon* crew—they'll be demoted if they murder anyone here."

She did smile, but made a cryptic statement. "You would like to see them demoted."

"I would?" said East, who could not see what that had to do with anything.

"How the rabble enjoys to see the mighty fall," said Estelita. "And they will do anything within their tiny grasp to make it happen."

5/25/225 Thea Estate,
Wilderness, Southern, Aeolis

Mercedes and Niki had retreated to his house in the Wilderness. They sat together on his narrow bed built into the wall. She had her legs folded beneath her and held his hurt foot in her lap. So far as she knew he had let no one else near it. He was still dressed, minus his jacket, and he was barefoot. He leaned back on the cushions that were scattered on the bed with the wide-woven afghans. He reached to the nightstand and swallowed a pill.

After trying to convince Niki to have his ankle repaired for the next performance, the conversation had lapsed, and Mercedes was feeling disturbed and comfortable and warm. It was pleasant here, sunbeams streaming in through two gabled windows with a chlorophyll-scented breeze and the lazy sound of bees. It was a small room with slanting ceiling like an attic for children to play in—and hide in. She could almost step outside herself and see the two of them together as they were. They *were* a pretty pair. She was feeling less innocent than she looked, but even desire seemed innocent. Niki was looking very very boyish and vulnerable.

"Mercedes, I—" he started, stopped, looked aside, considering how to proceed.

A breeze parted the pale-green curtains, and Niki's expression changed as if seeing an ill-timed visitor. "Out," he said.

The breeze went out.

Whether it was his own deep-running inhibitions he had seen or an inquisitive ghost, he did not get past it, and his thought went unspoken.

5/25/225 Oasis Port,

Desert of the Bells, Northern, Aeolis

When the crew of the *Halcyon* had sent the biopsy of the dragon for analysis, it was in an unlabeled freezer capsule because they did not want to label it "dragon biopsy." The researchers would figure out what it was soon enough and put a better label on it. But the reply, when it finally came, was baffling: We told you before, Mort information is classified.

Roxanna shook her head. *Maybe we don't know the rules. . . . Well, dammit, make up some new ones.* Then she knew.

She remembered the Mort analysis East had brought back—a humanoid with a half-set of animal chromosomes. So what was this dragon that the Service thought it was a Mort?

An animal with a full set of humanoid chromosomes.

"They're all the same," said Roxanna. "The Morts, the monsters . . . and they *are* coming out of thin air! *They've been here all along!*"

Returning natives were one thing, but natives that had never left were another. It was not a matter of money, but the land, the irreplaceable land. "It doesn't belong to us. None of it," Buddy whispered.

"Shall we get a message out?" Roxanna said to Per.

"To our benevolent superiors?" Per said acidly. "They probably *know*. They sent us down here blind, and I will bet you they knew from the *start* there were natives of some kind down here. They knew, they didn't tell us, and they didn't ask us if we were willing to risk our lives for this."

And none of them doubted that their lives were actually in

grave danger. Not from the native Aeolians—the natives had tolerated the Earthlings for 225 years. It was their own kind that would kill them. The landed aristocracy would never let them tell.

The crew was trying to stay calm, but Buddy broke first—just before the other two—and blurted out, "Let's get out of here."

Part Three:
WIND DANCER

Chapter I.
Eye of the Hurricane

5/25/225 Gem Theater,
Drina Village, New Europe, Northern, Aeolis

Not a sign of pain, not a trace of unsteadiness or of favoring one foot, as if transported beyond pain, beyond any physical need, for Niki there was only the dance. He had not had his ankle healed. He had even refused to take a painkiller since early morning, as if he needed all his senses intact to dance—even the sense of pain.

Once offstage, though, he walked immediately to his dressing room and shut the door. He sat with controlled weariness before the mirror—

And did not move an eyelash when the reflection of a kicked-dog of a boy-man formed in the glass.

Niki did not turn around, did not move, did not register shock, did not react at all. Yet there was recognition in the dark eyes—as one seeing a long-forgotten sin come home to roost.

Niki was not actually surprised, for he knew it had to come sometime, but there was no avoiding the sinking feeling when the time actually came. And Leader sensed revulsion.

Leader—who was no longer called Leader—had come to ask questions, but he sensed all the answers in Niki's stare, so there was nothing left to say but a warning.

137

But Niki was out of the room as fast as if changing into wind, for when he finally moved it was almost quicker than the eye could see. And he locked the dressing-room door, ignoring a voice trying to shout a warning after him. But it was only a whisper.

"There is a concert in five hours in Little Asia," said Niki to Mercedes outside the theater. "If I come for you then, will you be awake?"

"I'll be up," said Mercedes. Even if she had to use artificial sleep, she *would* be awake. "Won't you come to the chalet with me now?" She wondered if he would take that as a proposition. It was.

"No," said Niki. "I want to sleep for a while. I am going home."

5/25/225 *Oasis Port,*
Desert of the Bells, Northern, Aeolis

Apprehension and foreboding hung so heavily on Roxanna that she could barely function, her fingers shaking, her throat tight. She could not be gone from this planet fast enough, as in a dream, trying to run from a half-formed, nebulous horror, and getting nowhere.

She was strapped into her seat for liftoff, drumming her fingers on the console. *Get me out of here.*

A hand fell on her shoulder, and she almost shrieked, but it was only Buddy, who had unstrapped himself to come over and stop her damned finger-drumming.

Buddy reseated himself, and Roxanna drummed her toes within her boots.

The ship's hatches locked and sealed.

Can't we go any faster than this?

The pressure control was set, and the internal atmospheric system switched on. The hangar locks were taken up, the land engines started, and the ship's brakes lifted.

Per requested a launch site over the radio.

"Bay ten, *Halcyon*," came the answer.

"Bay ten, acknowledged."

"You are clear to taxi."

"Got it," said Per, and the *Halcyon* rolled out of the hangar.

Roxanna was beginning to breathe more normally, until the controller's voice came again. "Hold it right there, *Halcyon*."

Per braked and Roxanna forgot to breathe.

"Hold for a Kushuh shuttle crossing your path on track double alpha," the controller explained.

"Acknowledged," said Per, both rattled and relieved.

"Jesus!" said Roxanna, half prayer, half curse.

They waited. Finally the shuttle crossed in front of them. "We could've made that," said Roxanna.

"Will you please shut up!" said Per.

"Yes, sir," said Roxanna, and drummed her fingers.

"Proceed, *Halcyon*," said the controller.

"Acknowledged," said Per and started the *Halcyon* rolling again.

Please hurry, thought Roxanna. *Please, please hurry. They'll never let us out of here with what we know. Never. Never. Never.*

The *Halcyon* rolled into position on launch bay ten, and Per requested an exit passage through Aeolis's encircling energy field. He waited for the course to be fed into the ship's computer from the controller's computer.

"Um," said the ground controller.

Um? thought Roxanna. *Never. Never. Never.*

"*Halcyon*, could you move over to bay nine? We've got a traffic buildup along your intended trajectory. You can start to taxi."

"Acknowledged," Per growled and rolled the *Halcyon* down the track another two kilometers to bay nine. "Requesting a path and clearance for *Halcyon*," he said, once in position again.

Roxanna held her breath.

And held it.

And ran out of breath. *What is taking so long?*

The controller's voice spoke again. "Please hold, *Halcyon*."

"We *are* holding," Per snapped back, but Roxanna noticed he had not depressed the transmit switch.

Roxanna closed her eyes. It would have been so easy to escape had they just taken a public shuttle to Kushuh and left the *Halcyon* behind.

But what if they were wrong and no one was actually chasing them? She could hear their superiors: You left *what*, *where?*

But she knew they were not wrong. *If they catch us they'll never let us go.*

"*Halcyon XLV*," came the controller's voice. "Captain Per Safir, your request is denied. Please taxi back to hangar via track double queen."

"*Why?*" Per cried into the radio.

"I'm sorry," said the controller. "You and your crew are grounded by order of the duchess Estelita. I can't let you out."

Never. Never. Never.

5/25/225 Gem Theater,

Drina Village, New Europe, Northern, Aeolis

Leader tried not to panic. There were still a few minutes left to get his warning out. His hands fumbled with the lock on the door, but he could not decipher how the Earth contraption worked. He turned to his wind form and hurled himself at the walls of the dressing room, feeling for an opening.

It was airtight.

He incarnated again, shaking worse than before, and he pounded on the door with his fists. "Let me out! Let me out!" he whispered in broken English.

He heard foreign words spoken by someone on the other side. He recognized the word *clef*. That meant key, didn't it?

He heard leisurely footsteps retreat from the door. "Hurry!" Leader whispered.

The wait was interminable.

Leader glanced at a clock on Niki's dressing table. Fifteen minutes had passed. Leader knew how long that was—long enough for Niki to get anywhere in the world. To get home. Where the Outcast were waiting.

The leisurely steps returned with a rattling of keys. Leader heard the Earthling try one, then another, then fit the correct key into the panel.

"Ah," said the voice.

A gust of wind nearly knocked the startled stagehand over as the door flew open to an empty room.

Leader whistled out of the building and streaked to the sky, making the air crackle as he went. Then he stopped dead. He did not know where he was going. He hadn't an idea in the world of where Niki Thea lived.

5/25/225 *Oasis Port,*

Desert of the Bells, Northern, Aeolis

The *Halcyon* returned to the hangar as directed. There Per switched off the radio and turned to his two crewmates. He spoke low as if someone could overhear. "Split up. Don't tell each other what you are doing, just get off this planet the best way you know how. I'm going to stay here and cover for you. With luck they won't realize we've separated till you two are well away."

"Captain, if they get hold of you—" Buddy started.

"I trust you two will call in the cavalry before it gets to that," said Per. "Suicide is not what I had in mind. Now the sooner you get out of here, the sooner you can rescue me, right? So go."

"Yes, sir." Buddy saluted, opened the hatch, and jumped out.

Roxanna paused to lift Per's hat and plant a kiss on his blond head, then she scampered after Buddy.

"Thanks, Rox," she heard behind her.

5/25/225 *Thea Estate,*

Wilderness, Southern, Aeolis

Pale curtains parted to a malevolent current of air. Bare feet materialized and tiptoed across the floor, and anxious hands locked the windows and the door. A small injector was dropped by a funnel of air onto the carpet with a tiny thump that made the guilty ones start and look to see if they had wakened their prey.

They silently formed a semicircle around the narrow bed, then paused all at once, checked by awe. He was just a young male, asleep, but the Outcasts became afraid at the sight of him, as of a dormant god; and they might have gone away right then and left him alone, but Scorpii, who was in the back and was too short to see, pushed from behind. "Go on!"

And they did.

5/25-6/225 Oasis Port,
Desert of the Bells, Northern, Aeolis

Roxanna ran up to the shuttle bay, where passengers were boarding for Kushuh. She did not dare purchase a ticket from the machine, for that would require slotting her ID into the computer terminal. Instead she waited until she spotted a passenger who did not look like an aristocrat. Servants were used to being ordered. She waylaid the young man and explained to him in a very businesslike tone that she was confiscating his ticket. She said it was an emergency—which was true—then told him to go to the hangar where the *Halcyon* was berthed to collect a recompense and a free ticket on the next shuttle. She trusted Per would figure out what the situation was, for he would be expecting just about anything.

The servant was dismayed, but he did not complain too loudly. He surrendered his ticket and started off to find *Halcyon*'s hangar.

Roxanna took off her Service jacket, took off her hat and hid it in her jacket, and carried both in a bundle. She thanked God for her tartan vest and gold hairpins that made her look more civilian. She casually climbed the shuttle ramp, gave over her ticket, took her seat, and waited.

And drummed her fingers.

The last people boarded and the last call was given. The hatches were closed and all was secured for takeoff. The engines engaged, and Roxanna sank back in her seat, closed her eyes, and let go a sigh.

Then the engines wound down again—

No.

—and shut off.

Oh, no.

The hatch opened and two tall men marched up the aisle.

5/25-6/225 *Candle-in-the-Wind,*
Drina Village, New Europe, Northern, Aeolis

Mercedes relived a few memories in her mind as she waited for Niki at her chalet, from the first "You were lovely," to holding him when he fell, to a moment when she thought he would say . . . she was not sure what, but she knew she wanted to hear it.

She waited, nervous, blushing. And grew tired waiting.

She tried to read a book, stared at the words but assimilated nothing, put it down, looked at the chronometer on the wall, got up, went upstairs. She sat down before her mirror, tried on a different necklace, switched back to the pearls. She picked up a phone, put it down.

She lay across the bed and fell asleep.

She woke up, looked at the clock. She ran to the French doors, threw them open, and screamed to the wind, "Niki, you had better be dead!"

5/25-6/225 *Thea Estate,*
Wilderness, Southern, Aeolis

The entity sometimes called Leader swept into an open window, through the hallways, in and out of rooms of the strange house. He had found the right place. There were lives here, many hundred. They avoided the Outcast entity without communication—but also without commotion or alarm, and Leader wondered if it was possible that he had arrived in time. There seemed to be nothing amiss—nothing that the Ancient Ones who dwelled here were aware of.

Leader swept up the stairs, came to a room with the door ajar but all the windows locked, and, inside, a robot was stuffing bedding into its laundry bin, sweeping the carpet and purifying the air.

Another door down the hall was shut, and the sound of a running shower came from within.

Leader knew he was too late. The Outcast had come and gone. Hundreds of allies in the house, and all were unaware that they had been needed, and Niki evidently had not told them after it was over.

All Leader could hope now was that Niki's animal form was a white dog.

He materialized, feeling defeated. He sensed hostility from the living air, but also puzzlement as to what this Outcast could possibly be doing here. They had no idea what had happened under their roof.

Leader, feeling awkward, skinny, and naked, ventured into the bedroom, tugged an afghan away from the reluctant robot, and threw it around himself like a cloak. He went back out into the hall to wait for the shower to stop running. It was a long wait.

Niki emerged at last. Still damp, he wore his clothes carelessly. His usually smooth-parted hair was wet and uncombed. He was barefoot and he limped. His eyes were ringed blue from the drug. The winds whispered around him, *What's wrong, what's wrong, what's wrong?*

"Nothing. Go away. I ate something," Niki mumbled, brushing them aside. He seemed scarcely aware of Leader, but then looked straight at him with dilated eyes and said, "Do you have something to tell me? I will listen. I am much wiser than I was."

"No . . ." Leader stammered, wondering what he was still doing here, for his mission had failed. He felt he should explain, but he was daunted by the man's age, his height—for Niki was very tall for a Kistraalian—and his . . . *self.* "No, sir. I have nothing to say."

"Who are you?" said Niki.

"I . . . I was called Leader. I was called Pala before that. I am not called anything now. I . . . I was cast out . . . then the Outcast cast me out . . . no one talks to me now," he whispered, blinking hard, realizing his situation as he spoke it, facing the prospect of eternity alone.

"I will give you someone to talk to," said Niki, tired. "The Ancient Ones need a voice now that the Earthlings know. They asked me, but I'll not stay human much longer." His gaze turned inward. "No longer than it takes," he added sotto voce.

Leader stuttered, "Ancient Ones—talk to *me?*"

"You speak very badly, but you will have to do." Niki turned his head aside distractedly and looked through the open door to his room, which the robot had left clean, pleasant, and warm.

Leader could not tell what Niki saw as he looked in. Niki was noticing something missing that he could not quite pinpoint. A scent. Mercedes's perfume. It was gone now. He spoke again after a long pause. "I am sure the Ancient Ones will accept an outcast of the Outcast." He met Leader's eyes again. "How many Outcast are there?"

"Twenty-four—no, three—two—"

Niki waited.

"Twenty-one, plus me," Leader said finally.

"All of them female?"

"No, sir. Only seventeen."

"Seemed like hundreds," Niki murmured and went into his room.

Leader stood in the doorway, holding tight to the afghan, tense. He risked a question. "Were you born on Earth?"

"No. The Ancient Ones told me how to contaminate the memory of the Universal Bank. I told them to make up a genealogy for me going back to the 1600s and to make me wealthy. When this land went up for auction I bought the Wilderness—and graves for my friends. I have since become my own son and grandson."

When Aeolis had been up for auction . . . his own grandson . . . Niki had to be over two hundred years old, which was a very long time for beings whose humanoid form only lived forty years. "How did you live so long?"

"I am afraid to sleep," said Niki.

The wind form never slept. That was what made it unbearable for most—no rest, ever wakeful. Niki was ideally suited for such a life.

"I am afraid I will not wake up," he explained.

That kind of pessimism was the province of the Outcast. Leader did not see that Niki had any right to it. "That's fatalistic," he said.

"Fatalistic!" said Niki. "I saw the end of the world."

Leader's hands clutched. He could not breathe. "You . . ." His lips formed the word but could not speak what was too overwhelming, too impossible to be spoken. Finally he was able to say what Niki was *not*. "You are . . . not . . . a Young One."

Niki turned to him the eyes of a sphinx, ageless and infinite. "No."

He had seen Kistraal. He had seen. He had breathed a different atmosphere, walked on different grasses. Perhaps there had been birds, perhaps trees, and he had lived in a civilization that had been erased from the galaxy ten thousand years ago.

Leader sat down on the floor, stunned, staring.

"Fatalistic you do not know," said Niki. "You have never seen the world crumble—literally crumble—beneath you. Buildings fall, men and women turn to dust, forests collapse in a layer of black ash and wash into the sea with the rains. And it can happen again. The Earthlings will discover what the creature was—they want to know very badly—and they will recreate it. And maybe they will even house it in a laboratory on a geological fault as was done the first time."

There were tears on Leader's face. He made no sound.

"Do you actually think they would be any wiser than we were if they knew how to make such a weapon?"

"Do any of you know?" Leader whispered, chest tight.

Niki did not answer.

"I won't tell them," said Leader. "I am the only voice the Ancient Ones have, and I won't tell."

Niki still did not speak. He sat down at a small desk.

Leader craned his neck to see the desk top. "What are you writing?"

"My will," said Niki.

"You are dying?"

"I will never die. Long after all of you are dead, I will still be dancing. I and the Ones who made the portals and the arches. I am dying in that I will not return to this world for a very long time."

After a long silence Leader spoke again, a whispered prayer. "I hope there is a child."

"There will not be," said Niki.

"You are . . . a mule?"

"No."

"Then how can you know?"

"I was trapped in my sterile form."

Sterile form. Leader was confused. One's sterile form was one's animal form—the form one was not born in. He tried to make sense of it. "You weren't human-born?"

"I was," said Niki. "In my other human form. This one has the sprained ankle. The other danced tonight."

Leader stared. "But there is no such caste."

"I am older than the castes. I am the last of my kind."

Leader hid his face in his hands. "The Earthlings are wrong. There is no God."

"There is a God and it is dance, it is song, it is art. It is creation, not Creator." He got up from the desk and lay down on his bed. "Guard me?" he said.

"I promise," said Leader, numb. "Nothing will happen to you."

"Goodbye, then. Once I leave I shan't incarnate again until you are dead. I can outwait all of you." He closed his eyes and was immediately asleep. Leader covered him with an afghan.

It was quiet. Leader sat on the floor in the morning sunlight, his eyes shut.

A pair of inquisitive dark eyes appeared in the window. Leader opened his own eyes as shadow crossed his face. It was Leo.

Leader rose silently to his feet and opened the window. "What do you want?" he whispered.

"I want to see Niki," Leo whispered, eyes narrow in the daylight.

"Haven't you seen enough?" Leader said harshly.

"No, Leader, I didn't . . . I ran . . . so did Pega . . . it didn't seem right."

"You could be cast out for talking to me. And don't call me Leader."

"I don't care. Pega and I would rather stay with you."

Leader looked back over his shoulder. "Niki is asleep."

"I just want to look at him," said Leo, who would have been too frightened to say a word to Niki if he had a chance.

Leader stepped aside.

Leo did not even come in. He just gazed with the reverence of a pilgrim, then quietly left, looking as if he had witnessed a miracle in the disheveled dancer with blue-ringed eyes and damp hair.

Leader left the window open. Outside a hummingbird hovered about the flowers of a climbing vine in the morning calm.

Leader reseated himself on the floor, in the shade by the bed, until a rush of air swept through the curtains.

Niki was gone.

5/26/225 *Estate of the duchess Estelita,*
Little Asia, Northern, Aeolis

Roxanna was told that she was being taken to see the duchess. Roxanna did not feel honored.

The room to which she was admitted in the palace of the duchess was not a reception hall, but a small inner chamber, from which no cry for help could possibly reach outside. Roxanna noticed this and considered screaming before the door was shut behind her.

Her heart rose and sank in one beat to see two sheepish and familiar men held prisoner with her. Buddy and Per.

She saw hope bleed from their faces as they saw her. With an apologetic look, she walked over to stand with them.

Fear for her life diminished and she almost laughed when the duchess entered, flanked by twelve bronze, towering, well-muscled, armed men, tresses of gold hair flowing down her back, which was arched from the forward thrust of her chest.

She can't be serious.

"So," said Estelita by way of introduction. "You tried to leave my planet without telling me what you found here."

"We weren't told to report to you," Captain Safir replied, managing a reasonable tone. "Just to the Service, but I'm sure they'll send you a copy of the report as soon as it's—"

"It is by *my* authority that the Service is here," the duchess interrupted. "And I will know what you have discovered before you leave."

This woman is not real, Roxanna was thinking. *The dragon I can believe. This woman, I cannot. People cannot be this weird.*

"You found natives, didn't you?" said Estelita.

Roxanna's mind froze.

"Perhaps," Per evaded.

But Estelita would have none of *perhaps*. "By law a planet belongs to its intelligent natives and may not be confiscated or otherwise come into Earth possession without proper compensation and assent of its natives. Are you telling me that we do not own Aeolis?"

"No, ma'am—"

"Then I am telling you," said Estelita. "I saw a creature change from a pitiful excuse for a man into a worse excuse for a deer before my very eyes. Then I saw this creature disappear. There has always been a capricious wind on this world, Mr. Safir. And it has always hated me. You are not going to give my land over to *wind*."

"Are you sure they want it?" said Per. "If they have been here all this time and never tried to reclaim it, isn't that tantamount to assent? I'm sure once we establish communication with them they won't have any objection to our using their land."

"I'm not talking *use!*" Estelita said shrilly. "I am talking *ownership*." Ownership of land was the difference between serfs and aristocrats. The mark of aristocracy was, had always been, land.

"That can be worked out with the Aeolians," said Per.

"How do you know that?" said Estelita. "How do you know these are ignorant savages that will sell an island for a box of beads? Even if they are ignorant, your Service will not allow them to remain so. You will tell them their land is beyond price and you will tell them not to sell. That is what your Service will do, will it not?"

Per cleared his throat. "They will come up with an equitable decision—"

"No they will not," said Estelita. "*I* will." She turned to her attendants and jutted a finger at the Service officers. "Shoot!"

The guns raised and fired before any of the *Halcyon*'s crew could try to run, and a shrill voice sounded as blackness fell, "And I want to be rid of Lady Laure Remington's ugly bodyguard as well!"

5/26/225 Remington Estate, New Africa, Southern, Aeolis

Laure was sitting on a swing in the garden. She was wearing a white dress, daisies in her hair, and one daisy between two toes of a white-sandaled foot. She had wanted a dragon's tooth to wear around her neck, but the Service had confiscated the whole dragon. Laure was not used to being told no, and she was not fond of the Service.

"What are your Service friends doing now?" Laure asked her bodyguard. She was too sly for it to be a casual question.

East was seated high atop the garden wall, one foot on the wall, one dangling off the side, his gun across one knee. "I haven't heard from them," he said.

"With all they have to go on now, if they've not come up with anything, they can't be very bright. Perhaps they'll never find out what is happening here and you won't ever leave." Her veiled innuendoes were becoming steadily bolder. East was not certain what her game was this time. Whatever it was, East was not playing—not by her rules, anyway. "Actually," he said, "I think they *have* discovered what they're looking for."

Laure was clearly surprised and not very happily. "What makes you think that?"

"Because I haven't heard from them."

Laure's brow furrowed. "Wouldn't they tell you?"

"No."

Laure was holding onto the ropes, leaning back in the swing, her head thrown back to look up at him. "That doesn't bother you?"

East could do very well without the Service. "I can fend for myself."

"And me," said Laure, bolder still. "East, if you were stranded in the middle of a jungle with no conveniences at all, could you survive?"

"Yes."

Her face took on a wistful adventurous look. "I don't know if I could."

Of course you could. You're not the lap dog your husband is. Then it struck East what she was saying. It was possible to read too much into it, but going out into the wilds would mean abandoning Stephen. Was she making a tentative offer?

They were looking at each other in a standoff, she on the swing, he on the wall.

East looked away first, eyes drawn by two intruders he spied stealing up the garden walk behind the tall hedges. It was their very stealth that attracted his attention. Had they walked normally he would not have noticed them.

Laure turned and followed his gaze. Her brows lowered and her expression went from teasing challenge to annoyance to serious concern. There was no servant accompanying the two visitors. "East—"

The two men saw that they had been sighted, and suddenly guns appeared.

East jumped down to Laure as a beam of energy burned the top of the wall where he had been. *Beam guns!* He seized Laure from the swing and dragged/carried her into a shallow gully in the brush behind an outcropping of rock as he returned fire with his projectile gun.

The intruders, dodging East's fire, were not sure exactly where the quarry had gone once the shooting stopped, and they approached the area cautiously, staying close to trees for protection.

A tree would not shield East from a beam gun—not much would—if they could find him.

East whispered to Laure, "Is there any way to circle behind them?"

Laure frowned, then brightened. She crawled along the embankment to a hidden robot maintenance panel.

And robots began to pop up from their tunnels and skitter through the brush.

One of the men pointed to a movement in the bushes, and they both blasted the little robot out of existence. They ran to see what they had hit, when they sighted another movement and blasted that.

East shook his head, amazed.

Then Laure sent a robot down the walk on the far side of the hedge. East knew at once what she was doing. *If you can't get behind them, make them turn their backs.* It was pure Laure.

As soon as both men turned toward the movement with their guns pointed at the robot, East stood up, shot one in the back, and caught the other turning. He had no qualms about a shot in the back when dealing with beam guns.

Laure came out of the brush and put her arms around his waist. Primitive men were to be controlled by primitive methods, so as the lioness does the work and surrenders the kill to the male, Laure took no credit for her own ingenuity. "What would I do without you?"

"Breathe a lot easier," said East. "They weren't after you.

They wanted me." The first beam scores were on the wall, not the swing.

"*Why?*"

"There's something that damned *Halcyon* isn't telling me," he said. "Go back to the house, call the police, and have them protect you. I'm worse than useless to you now."

"No, I'm going with you. Where are you going?"

"Laure, you're hugging a bull's-eye. I'm hired to protect you, and the best way I can do that now is to stay well away."

"All right. You're fired. I'm going with you."

"Dammit, woman—"

"You know better than to argue with me, Mr. East," she said. "Besides, how far do you think you can get without me?"

That much he could not argue with. There was no way of getting anywhere without the lady's assistance.

"Where are we going?" she asked.

"Oasis."

She took his hand. "This way."

"The house is that way."

"I know where my house is," said Laure. "We're not taking a tube shuttle. They are too easy to stop."

She led him to the private hangar. As they neared, they sighted two more men bearing beam guns, and they broke into a run.

Laure and East bolted into the hangar and locked the door. They could hear beam guns burning through the metal walls. The beams would pierce through in a matter of seconds.

There were three ships in the hangar, all with *LaFayette* emblazoned on the walls. Laure chose the one that had seen the eye of a hurricane, the ship *Windhover*. They boarded as the beam guns cut through the hangar wall.

East reached to the dial that would open the doors to the taxi rails that led to the launch site, but Laure stayed his hand. "Don't even think it." She engaged the engines as a beam seared the surface of the ship's hull, and she blasted off, crashing through the hangar's thin roof to open sky.

5/26/225 Oasis Port,

Desert of the Bells, Northern, Aeolis

When Laure made an illegal entry into Oasis with her beam-scored ship, the police chief, Luis Del Fuego, was there to meet her.

"Señora, you look as if you have been in battle!" said the handsome caballero.

Laure paid him no heed. She was staring into an empty hangar where the *Halcyon* should have been. "East, they've gone."

But East was not so certain. He had a feeling the *Halcyon* had not left Aeolis. He had a tracker with him, but it had a limited range and he had nothing to key on. There was no way to key in a Douglas tartan.

"Señora, señor," Del Fuego said, "you are in trouble. What can I do for you?"

East spoke, "A ship. The United Earth Serviceship *Halcyon XLV*. Where is it?"

"*Halcyon?*" Del Fuego repeated, frowning in thought. "One moment, señor, I shall check. *XLV*, you say?"

"How many halcyon-class ships come through here that you wouldn't remember this one?" East demanded impatiently.

"There are many ships in Oasis, señor. I do not recall one *Halcyon XLV*. I do not recall a halcyon ship of any number. Come into my office and I will check."

Laure and East followed Del Fuego down the concourse to the police station. They went into the office, and Del Fuego shut the door. He rang up a list of ships in port on his computer screen. "There is no *Halcyon* in Oasis. Nor, señor, has there ever been one."

Laure spoke, "How much are you being paid to forget you ever saw that ship?"

The caballero smiled with brilliant white teeth. "The same am being paid to forget the señor." He drew his gun on East—started to—but East was familiar with that motion, saw it coming long in advance, kicked the gun from his grasp and caught him on the chin with his fist.

The police chief dropped and did not get up.

"Is he dead?" Laure bent over the collapsed form.

"I didn't hit him that hard. Aeolians fold easy," said East flatly. "But I can tell you who *is* dead." He pictured a short, blondish Swede, a bedimpled Asian, and an auburn-haired, bagpipe-blowing pain in the teeth.

"Maybe not," said Laure. "I think I know who is after you. Knowing her, she might not have killed your friends yet. If she hasn't, I know where to look."

5/26/225 Babylon,

Little Asia, Northern, Aeolis

Roxanna was surprised to awaken and find that she had been drugged or stunned, not killed. She should have rejoiced, but could not.

Not in a gladiator's pit.

Her murder had merely been postponed. And now, instead of terrified, she was angry, because it was like being made to die twice, and that was an experience that should be endured only once. Twice was simply not fair. She had believed with all her being that she was dying the first time in the duchess's chamber. She had nearly vomited from sheer horror, but she had passed out too quickly to do anything at all. Darkness had overcome her for what she had been convinced was the last time. To find out that it was not the last time gave her the feeling that she had been cheated, and that she was living on borrowed time. It lent a sense of invincibility. She could not be hurt because she was already dead.

She was naked like the gladiator facing her. The spectators liked an abundance of skin showing so they could see the blood more clearly when a gladiator was wounded.

Roxanna's opponent was a man, brown and wiry, like a Thai boxer.

Each of them had been given a short blunt dagger that was good for little but tearing skin and drawing blood for the audience to drool at.

The duchess was reclining at the edge of the pit on a litter held by six musclebound attendants. And all around the pit were the impeccably dressed bloodthirsty aristocrats.

Per and Buddy were in cages in a subcellar, awaiting their turn to fight—to die, for the outcomes of these matches were forgone conclusions, the duchess having made certain that the *Halcyon*'s crew was hopelessly overmatched.

Roxanna's turn was first. She faced the wiry man, exhortations, hisses, and torments filling her ears. She felt the blunt knife in her hand, which she was expected to use to draw her opponent's blood as he killed her.

But she was too incensed to do what what was expected of her. Instead of lunging, stabbing, and parrying, she blessed Per for ever teaching her to throw a dart, and she hurled her knife across the pit into the lean man's throat. Then she picked up his dropped blade and threw it as hard as she could at the indolent figure reclining on the litter.

Estelita screamed, a trickle of blood flowing from a small cut over her right eyebrow, a lump forming.

Missed!

Estelita rose to her feet, shrieking, "Kill her! Kill her! Kill her!" She pointed at the naked girl in the pit, and the attendants drew guns to obey, but then Estelita barked. "No! Slowly. Do it slowly."

Roxanna's face remained proudly impassive, to Estelita's greater fury. The duchess clutched at one of her lackey's muscled arms. "Kill the other two first. Make her watch."

And Roxanna's bravado caved in. She had forgotten that there were worse things than dying twice.

5/26/225 *Windhover*

In transit over the northern continent, East sent an SOS from the *Windhover* on the Service phase-jumper channel to any Service ship that might be near the Aeolian solar system. He was surprised to make contact—with an entire squadron within the same phase. He had expected a minimum of five beats to the return signal. There were no beats at all. They had to be within the solar system, standing by.

Standing by for what?

Damn you, you expected this!

"We need assistance," East told them. "The ship *Halcyon XLV* has been seized illegally by the Aeolian government, the status of the crew is uncertain, and *I* have been shot at. Do you copy?"

"Affirmative, *Windhover*," came the answer without surprise, without question. "We can give you an assist in thirty-six standard hours."

"Thirty—" East sputtered. "Where the hell are you? You sound like you're right on top of me."

The reply came without beats. "Affirmative, *Windhover*. We are on Kushuh. Thirty-six hours is the minimum time to pass screening and sterilization for entry into Aeolis's atmosphere."

They were already here and mobilized, expecting, and they could not move any faster than that. That was the Service. "Screw sterilization," said East. "In thirty-six hours we'll all be dead."

"Sorry, *Windhover*. Thirty-six hours it is. We cannot jeopardize the whole planet."

"Dammit, we need help *now*!" East shouted and punched in the radio with his fist.

Laure was sitting beside him, disconcerted. "You killed my radio."

"If I live, you may deduct it from my pay," East said in anger.

Laure pouted at his gruffness. The woman did not have the sense to be afraid.

Suddenly she sat on the edge of her seat and pointed down. "There it is. Babylon."

5/26/225 Babylon,

Little Asia, Northern, Aeolis

The restaurant that stood over the gladiators' den was closed, and there was no one about to become alarmed at the *Windhover*'s descent or at East's armed approach, though he knew his arrival had been monitored and that a suitable reception would be waiting for him down below. He ordered Laure to stay outside with the ship. She did not argue, and he was too preoccupied to mark how very unlike her it was.

He traced down the corridors and stairs and elevators till he reached the final door. In what was certainly suicide—but it would be unlike East to sit and wait for a death that was coming anyway—he crashed into the cellar with a flying kick and grabbed the nearest Aeolian to him as a shield, then he looked to see how he stood. He saw the duchess's bleeding forehead and Roxanna in the pit with a dead opponent. That, he guessed, was why his entrance had not been met with a spray of beams and bullets—no one had been watching the outside monitors.

Lords and ladies were screaming and scurrying for the corners as the lackeys produced guns and squared off for battle.

The duchess spoke to East. "You saved us the trouble of hunting you down." She motioned to her attendants. "Throw him in the pit."

But it was not East who was thrown, and what the fall did not take care of, Roxanna did.

There was a spatter of gunfire and shrieking, and East bellowed, "Roxanna, stay down!"

"How the hell do you think I'd get up?" Roxanna shouted from the pit as bullets and beams flew over. She took up one of her victim's guns. Unable to shoot anyone directly from her angle, she shot at the ceiling and brought large pieces down over the lackeys' heads.

East hit his repeater and stopped aiming, just fired to keep everyone down—and from taking aim at him. His shield slumped against him, shot or fainted. He released the body and rolled behind the bar and seized another Aeolian, a curly-haired youth who bit, scratched, and kicked East in the knee where his new leg had been joined on. Pain shot through him, and, with a head that felt full of cotton, he thought the leg would reject. It would no longer support his weight.

Amid beams flashing and the duchess shrilling, above it all, a voice like a clarion cried, "Stop!" It was not the dutchess's screeching, but clear and loud without hysteria, a command that had to be obeyed—at least by East, for it was Laure's voice.

All shooting ceased. There were five dead on the floor, three in the pit.

The duchess raged in the silence, "Who are you taking orders from?" But none of the lackeys was willing to resume fighting. "I rule here!"

"No, you don't," Laure sang out, striding into the center of the cellar. "The winds rule here. They always have and always will."

"What are you raving about, child? You are standing in the line of crossfire."

East too was angry that she had defied him, but it was not in her character not to, and he could not stay too angry. East was barely on his feet, pained and hard pressed for breath, and when Laure had come striding into this hellpit, dressed in white, the light fighting timbre of her voice overriding the chaos, she appeared as an angel, as a tigress, and she was beautiful. *We may go down in flames, but God I love her.*

"My name is Laure Eva Aeolia. I am the first Earth child born on this world. The winds call me their own. Stop this or I shall have you all swept away."

"That is a lot of wind," said Estelita.

"Yes it is. An awful lot of wind. Look where you are before you move."

Uneasy glances shifted about the den, then someone looked at the outside monitors and uttered a muffled scream, seeing what she meant—where they all were.

In the eye of a hurricane.

"Stop them!" the duchess shrilled.

"We can't, your grace. We don't know what started them."

Estelita stared at Laure, outraged. "You *dare*—"

"Yes I do," Laure said merrily.

"Kill her," Estelita commanded.

But no one would.

"Kill who?" came a voice from the pit. It was Roxanna, with a beam gun trained on Estelita's head.

"Don't do it, Roxanna," said East tiredly. He had sunk to the floor and was holding his knee. On his arm was a bleeding beam score he didn't even know he had received. "You'll be demoted."

The duchess's remaining attendants looked from the monitors, to Laure, to their dead companions, to Estelita. And one by one they dropped their weapons into the pit with Roxanna, who did not shoot but did not lose her aim either.

Estelita was in a towering speechless rage. The aristocrats in the corners were cowering and whining, terrified of the awesome winds. "What are we to *do?*"

"I don't know." Laure shrugged. "Ask *them*."

There was a glimmering in the air in a clear space by the pit, and there materialized a small humanoid whom some of them recognized and whose presence made them even more frightened.

The small naked boy-man shifted nervously, squinting in the light. He had been here before. He spoke in whispering broken English, "I am called Speaker. I am the voice of the Ancient Ones. Whom should I speak to?"

Chapter II.
Legacy

Roxanna was sitting sullenly, her arms crossed, in an office with her crewmates and East. With the coming of the Service squadron—thirty-six hours late—an ambassador to Aeolis had been appointed, Estelita had been arrested, Del Fuego had been arrested, and Roxanna and East were under investigation for the lives they had taken, though they were assured there was nothing to worry about.

Roxanna was sure of nothing. She sat and scowled across the desk at her smooth-talking superior, who had much explaining to do.

"We knew we were sending you into a crisis zone," he admitted to the crew of the *Halcyon*. "We suspected there might be intelligent natives, but we had no hard evidence. We were hoping we could learn from what you sent us while keeping you safely ignorant. But you were more resourceful than we gave you credit for. And it is too bad a civilian was involved."

"I'll say," said East.

"You made out all right," Roxanna snapped. East had been given a new leg—put on correctly, this time—at Service expense, which was considerable.

"We regret that we were unable to respond to your SOS sooner. There was simply too much at stake on this planet."

"It's a good thing the Kistraalians didn't know that," said Roxanna wryly. "All they wanted of it were some grave plots."

"Make no mistake. We were honestly concerned for you—"

160

"Sure," said Roxanna, as she got to her feet and walked out, not caring if they court-martialed her.

Per and Buddy caught up with Roxanna later and handed her a message. She thought it was a summons, but it was her new ship assignment. "No promotion, I assume," she said.

"No," said Buddy. "The uniform would clash with your tartan."

Roxanna stepped on his foot. She looked over her assignment. "They're splitting us up," she said dully. She had not thought she would be sorry, but she was.

"Have to," said Buddy. "The *Halcyon* was destroyed."

"Everything I owned was on that ship," Roxanna moaned. "It's a good thing my bagpipes were already smashed or I'd really be mad."

Buddy and Per glanced at each other. "Ah . . . we got you a going-away present—" said Buddy.

"—seeing how we won't be around to listen to it any-more—" said Per.

"—you can play 'em till you're blue in the face."

"You didn't," said Roxanna.

6/4/225 *Candle-in-the-Wind,*

Drina Village, New Europe, Northern, Aeolis

Mercedes clung to a wet pillow and cried. She would never as long as she lived understand. Gone. Just suddenly gone without a word. And with him he took the dance, for there was no one to take his place. Mercedes and the troupe had remained on Aeolis in faint hope—growing fainter as the week passed—that Niki would show up. But it was evident that he had disappeared again. For a long long time.

And Mercedes went to sleep crying. And cried in her sleep.

Suddenly the windows burst open with great gusts of air. Mercedes woke with a scream, covered her head with her arms and cried, "Don't hurt me."

The winds stormed about the room, breaking a few things, but they did not disturb even a lock of her hair.

She felt a human hand on her shoulder and heard a voice. "Don't be afraid. They said you wanted to say goodbye. I never think to."

Mercedes peered from behind her sheltering arms. It was dark, and she saw Niki dimly. He was kneeling on the floor at her bedside. He wore nothing. She was too numb to think anything of it or how he had gotten in.

"I am leaving," he said. "I shan't be back. Not for a long time. Don't wait." He turned his head to gaze out the open window. His face looked very young. He turned back to her. "They said I could marry you."

"I would, whatever you are," said Mercedes.

"No. Humans should consort with humans."

She seized his hand. "Where are you going?"

"With them." He made a small motion with his head.

"Stay with me!" She cried on his hand, laid her cheek against his palm.

"I cannot. I do not want to grow old. Look at this." He pointed to three tiny lines in his forehead that were not even visible in the dim light, the night smoothing away all trace of age. "When did I get these? I never had them."

"Look at these," Mercedes returned, pointing at the circles under her eyes. "You gave me these."

"When you die, if you don't go to heaven or hell or wherever humans go, join me, if you can."

"Niki, do the winds ever die?"

"Only when they want to."

"Then where do they go?"

"No one knows. Maybe there is nothing. I don't want to know. I will never die."

Mercedes was sobbing. "Niki, before you go, would you kiss me?" When he hesitated, she cried fiercely, "No, forget it. I don't want to."

Niki's gaze fell, looking bewildered—and hurt. He did not say anything.

Mercedes put her arms around his neck and touched her lips to his. He did not actually kiss her back, but he did not draw away.

Mercedes felt his hand touch her face, thought he might crawl in bed with her, then suddenly her arms were empty and he was gone with a rush of cold air.

The winds howled out of the room. Mercedes sprang out of bed, ran to the window, and called his name, for she could think of nothing else to do—but cry.

5/6/225 Remington Estate,

New Africa, Southern, Aeolis

With a whole clan of LaFayettes congregated in the house, East escaped out to the verandah, where he found Laure. She did not smile. "Is Stephen letting you go?" she said.

She knew the answer to that one. She was just having trouble accepting it.

East nodded. "I'm not needed anymore." *As if I ever was. What ever gave Stephen the idea that you needed protecting?*

The lady's eyes were searching. "You promised you wouldn't leave me."

"I promised I wouldn't leave you alone," said East.

"You know, I think I *could* survive in a jungle," said Laure.

East felt something like skyrockets. But he could not be sure of her intent. Was she actually offering to come with him? She would not come out with it openly. And, not sure if he was being noble or cowardly, East did not ask her. She might say no, and East never gambled with stakes higher than he could afford to lose.

Someone came onto the verandah to call them inside, where Laure's grandfather was proposing a toast. *My God, this man is younger than I am. Time to go, East. Time to go.*

East did not hear the toast, but he drank to it—quite a bit.

Laure's father was expounding on "the lesson of Aeolis," as the others nodded, beginning with the fact that the natives did not know God, and winding up with their sorry end, deriving from that a morality tale that sounded worse and worse as East became steadily more drunk. Finally he exploded, "You think this entire planet and its people were put here as a lesson for Earth? What are you worth that a world should be created and destroyed for you? There's no lesson here. It's nothing but a tragedy, and you're a flock of vultures if you think there's anything to be picked out of it for you." He set down his glass and walked out of the house for the final time.

He heard quick light steps behind him as Laure trotted after him and took his arm. "East, you were splendid."

"I just took down your father and insulted your whole family," said East.

"They'll live. You were right. I'll miss you, East."

"I'll miss you," he admitted.

"I have to stay with my husband, don't I? Or you wouldn' think very much of me, would you?" There was a teasing glint in her eyes. She had never been so brazen.

East would not give her a straight answer. "Who am I to disapprove of you? I'm not your father."

"You keep saying that," she said. "As if it made any differ ence. You're not my lover either."

That was cruel and it hurt, and he told her so.

"I know," she said. "I just wanted to make sure you hur too. I don't like to suffer alone. Goodbye, East."

6/7/225 Oasis Port,
Desert of the Bells, Northern, Aeolis

Roxanna marched up and down the concourse with he bagpipes to a rousing melody and *thrum*, until a voice at he elbow said, "Roxanna, I never knew that you had freckles."

Squawk.

She didn't—on her face. Roxanna blushed down to he freckles. Just because she had been naked in the pit did no mean he had to look at her.

The bagpipes deflated with a dissonant sigh. "What do yo want, East?"

"I thought you would like to know that you and I hav been cleared. We're free to go," said East. "Estelita has bee sentenced."

"To what?"

"She's lost her land, she's lost her title, and she's been en listed in the Service. Estelita, servant of the people."

"She'll never do it," said Roxanna.

"She's under the same commander I was. She'll do as she told."

Roxanna took a breath. "I guess it's all over now," she sai and pursed her lips. It was hard to believe.

A piece of paper was swirling at their feet in an eddy air.

Litter! Here? East picked it up and unfolded it carefully s as not to smudge the markings. It was in scientific, the closest Earth came to a universal language, written out longhand, clear and studied, as if by a hand unused to it.

"What is it?" said Roxanna.

East was silent, scowling at it. At last he said slowly, "This is it."

"This is *what*?" said Roxanna.

"What killed them—the Kistraalians."

"*What?*"

East held up the paper. "How to destroy the world in one hundred and fifty-six easy steps. How to make a microorganism."

"Are you serious?"

"Perfectly."

Roxanna reached for it. "It was meant for me. I'm a Service officer, you're a civilian."

East snatched it from her reaching hand. "No. It's addressed to me."

It was. By his first name. *How did he find that out?*

"Why you? There are more responsible people."

"I believe I sparred with this gentleman once before."

Everyone is fundamentally evil. The good merely lack opportunity.

There was no doubt in East's mind that he had not been speaking to a human—not that harnessed chaos. Not a man, a wind dancer, and now East found himself caught up in a dance, the kind in which fire was thrown and swords flashed, and woe betide the dancer who missed a step.

"Who would I sell this to?" he mused.

"*East!*"

"It's worth anything I could ask for."

"Are you mad? That weapon backfired once already. Destroy it."

"I'm a mercenary," he said. "We all have to go somewhere—and my time is coming up quicker than yours. I may as well go in style."

Laure would be able to tell if he meant it. Roxanna couldn't. But she knew it could change anyone to hold in his hand the price of *anything*, wealth, title, land, entrance into the Aeolian class, Laure's class. She hovered at East's side, anxious.

Finally East addressed himself, "East, you were born to lose. You may be good, but you're very stupid."

Roxanna sighed in relief.

East looked down at her, resigned. "Since you and I are destined to be poor all our lives, Commander Douglas, shall we go to bed together, get drunk, gamble away what money we still have, or start a fight in a bar?"

Roxanna hooked his arm with the one of hers not holding the bagpipes. "One of those."

East paused to fold the paper, smearing the words to total illegibility, making it into a paper airplane. Then he tossed it back to the winds.

Rebecca M. Meluch graduated from the University of North Carolina at Greensboro with a B.A. in drama. She has worked as everything from a control clerk and keypunch operator to an assistant in the Classics department at Greensboro, and she has been active in nonprofessional theater. Her first novel, SOVEREIGN, is also available in a Signet edition. Miss Meluch lives in Westlake, Ohio.